"Abby?"

A voice jerked her out of her thoughts.

She was sure she was dreaming as the figure broke through the fog and she got a clear view of him.

It was him. Standing there like the answer to all the questions she'd been asking herself. For a moment, she just stared at him, her mouth hanging open. And then she snapped her jaw shut and said, "Paul."

Paul's handsome face broke out into a smile—so familiar, but different at the same time. His eyes crinkled in places they didn't before, but his hair was still that unruly shock of gold, dipping into his bright blue eyes.

"I'm sorry. I didn't mean to scare you."

He held out his arms and she stepped forward into them, letting him hug her. He smelled like the orchard, like green fresh leaves and summer, of memories she'd tried to avoid and promises she'd broken.

She closed her eyes, breathing it all in, trying to calm her thundering heart. She had nothing to fear from Paul.

Except her own damn weakness.

By Tess Diamond

BE A GOOD GIRL
SUCH A PRETTY GIRL
DANGEROUS GAMES

BE A
GOOD GIRL

TESS
DIAMOND

AVONBOOKS

An Imprint of HarperCollinsPublishers

BE A GOOD GIRL. Copyright © 2018 by Supernova, LLC. All rights reserved. Printed in the United States of America. No part of this book may be used or reproduced in any manner whatsoever without written permission except in the case of brief quotations embodied in critical articles and reviews. For information, address HarperCollins Publishers, 195 Broadway, New York, NY 10007.

First Avon Books mass market printing: April 2018

Print Edition ISBN: 978-0-06-265584-4
Digital Edition ISBN: 978-0-06-265585-1

Cover design by Nadine Badalaty
Cover photograph ©Mark Owen/Arcangel

Avon, Avon & logo, and Avon Books & logo are registered trademarks of HarperCollins Publishers in the United States of America and other countries.
HarperCollins is a registered trademark of HarperCollins Publishers in the United States of America and other countries.

FIRST EDITION

18 19 20 21 22   QGM   10 9 8 7 6 5 4 3 2 1

For my grandmother,
who always watched old noir movies with me.

ACKNOWLEDGMENTS

Thank you to Nancy Fischer and Beth Atwood for their ninja word skills and Shailyn Tavella for her enthusiasm. Huge thanks to Elle Keck and Tessa Woodward for their continued support.

PROLOGUE

Fifteen years ago

She felt numb. Like her entire body had been shot up with Novocain. Her arms lolled to the side as he carried her like a doll through the orchard. She could see the thick green leaves of the olive trees above her, her eyes drifting shut every few seconds.

She was so tired.

His face swam in and out of her fuzzy vision as she felt the ground against her back. He was setting her down.

Run, her mind said. But her body couldn't obey. She couldn't even lift her pinky. Every muscle felt locked in place, paralyzed, her limbs useless. She kept trying to move, tears tracking down her face as she struggled in vain.

He began to hum, his palm cradling the back

of her head gently as he pulled her double braids up and over her shoulders.

The gentleness made fear spike in her, adrenaline filling her body, her legs unable to respond.

He smiled.

"It's all right, sweet thing," he cooed at her, like she was a puppy. "It's better this way. You're serving a purpose." His smile grew wide. "You're my lesson."

He drew away from her, and all she could see were the branches of the trees and the pieces of sky and stars between them.

The trees were beautiful, she thought. So beautiful. At least she was here, in the trees.

As his hands closed around her throat, her eyes slipped shut.

And never opened again.

CHAPTER 1

The second she came into view of the cell block, the hooting and hollering started.

Abby's stomach twisted, a reactive response that almost any woman had when getting catcalled, but being in the prison intensified the stress. She refused to show it, squared her shoulders, and stared straight ahead. Keeping her face a smooth mask, she followed the guard down the narrow hall of the block. Cells lined both sides of the hall, prisoners pressing against the bars as they craned to catch a glimpse of her. For some of them, she was their first look at a woman on the block in years, maybe even decades. It wasn't often that Pinewood Correctional Facility let journalists inside general population, let alone solitary confinement.

But that was exactly where she was headed. She'd been a tight ball of nerves—a mix of fear and anticipation—since she'd gotten the call.

He had finally consented to see her. It had taken over a year and at least fifty letters, but she'd made it happen.

Her daddy always did say she was a determined girl. She'd grown up to be an even more determined woman.

And she was going to get what she wanted. What she *needed*.

"Stay close," Stan, the guard said, casting a glance at a prisoner pounding on the bars as they passed. Abby adjusted her stride so she was just within a step of him. She was a tall woman, with curvy hips and muscle tone on her arms that came from hauling hay bales instead of the gym. Coming home five years ago had meant going back to her roots—quite literally. When she'd arrived, her father's almond orchard was in dire need of some TLC, and she'd put the work in, on top of caring for him. When he'd passed away two years ago, he'd passed knowing the orchard was back to flourishing. She hoped it eased his mind. He had always been a hard man to please.

When she and Stan reached the end of the cell block, he opened the barred door, ushering her into another hallway. The silence of this part of the prison was abrupt and strange after the noise of the cell block, and it took Abby a moment to adjust as she walked alongside him.

"You okay?" Stan asked, looking at her, his gray eyebrows drawn together with concern. "I know they say some filthy stuff."

She smiled reassuringly at him. "I can handle it," she said.

"So is this visit for a new piece?" he asked, opening another door with his ring of keys. "I read that story you did, the one about that heroin addict. I liked it. Thought you did a good job, showing how the addiction was a disease and how we need to approach the drug problem like an epidemic."

"Thank you," Abby said. Normally, she'd be delighted her work had affected him, but her mind was on other things. On the man somewhere in this prison, who held answers to questions that had haunted her for years. "That's so nice of you to say. And I'm afraid I can't give any details about my works-in-progress. Contracts, you know." She shot him another smile, hoping he'd drop it.

Luckily, at that moment, they came to a stop in front of a thick steel door that had SOLITARY CONFINEMENT stamped on it.

Abby took a deep breath, her eyes settling on the words. This was it. In just minutes, she'd be face-to-face with him. Her heart was hammering in her chest at the thought.

She turned back to Stan, and was surprised at how troubled the older man looked.

"Are you sure about this?" he asked her.

"I'm a big girl, Stan," she said. "You don't have to worry about me."

"Look . . ." He licked his lips, looking nervous. "He's tricky. Really tricky."

"I've heard the rumors," Abby said.

She didn't need the rumors. She knew from real life exactly how sick the man she was about to meet was. She had spent the last two years learning everything there was to know about him. She'd talked to every teacher he'd ever had, every relative who was willing to speak to her and not slam the door in her face. She'd talked to every single person who'd even had a modicum of contact with Howard Wells, better known as Dr. X.

She knew him. And she was about to use that knowledge to get what she wanted from him.

"I just want you to be careful," Stan said. "He knows exactly what to say to get to you."

"I know he talked an inmate into killing himself," Abby said.

"Not just one," Stan said quietly, looking over his shoulder nervously before lowering his voice and adding, "And not just inmates."

Abby's eyes widened at the implication. She

knew she should press Stan for more information, but she also knew she could ferret out the truth herself with a little research. She didn't want to make him even more nervous, especially because he was authorized to cut her meeting short if he deemed the situation unsafe.

"I appreciate your concern," she told Stan. "But I'll only be asking him questions."

"Okay," Stan said. "Just don't get too close." He took her through the same rundown she'd gotten when she'd first entered the prison: no contact, no passing the prisoner anything, and no getting within even ten feet of the prisoner. Abby had a feeling that the last one was a specific rule for the man she was about to see.

The solitary wing was quiet as they walked through it to the very end, where a door led to another, even more isolated section.

"Inmate 3847, your visitor is here," Stan called out. Abby's skin prickled at the change in his voice. When talking with her, he had been kind, almost grandfatherly. But now, his voice was stern and authoritative, full of "don't fuck with me" attitude.

"You sit here," Stan said, pointing his baton at the bench set a good ten feet away from the thick, clear plastic wall that made up the front of Howard's cell. "Inmate 3847, come forward."

There was a pause, and Abby had to bite the inside of her cheek as he shuffled into view.

Howard Wells was fifteen years older than the last time she'd seen a picture of him, but he was no less terrifying. Goose bumps—the dreadful, horror-filled kind—spread across her skin as his eyes met hers.

His hair was gray now, slicked back, the comb tracks visible, like he'd carefully groomed it for this meeting. His orange jumpsuit was clean and tidy, his bright blue eyes shining in his craggy face.

His feet were shackled, but instead of his hands being cuffed, he was in a straitjacket, his arms lashed to his sides. Despite this, he held himself like he was the emperor of his own tiny kingdom. Like she was a serf who had the honor of experiencing his presence.

Abby showed no emotion as she sat down, placing her notebook and pen in her lap. Stan hovered in the corner, and Abby gave him a small nod.

"I'll be right outside," he said. "Panic button is right here." He pointed meaningfully at the red button on the wall. "Don't try any of your manipulative shit, Wells."

A light *tsk*ing sound filled the air as Stan left them alone, and Abby stared at him. He came forward, so he was just inches behind the thick sheet of Plexiglas that kept him from going for her. "Abigail Winthrop," he said.

"Hello, Howard," she said. She refused to call him Mr. Wells. And she certainly wasn't going to call him *Doctor*. There wasn't going to be any deference here.

She wasn't playing his game. She was here for answers—and she was going to get them.

"You've been very persistent," he said, looking her up and down, his mouth twisting in a way that made her stomach churn. She felt assessed, like a piece of meat, an object. But she stamped the nausea down.

That's what he wanted her to feel.

"As I said in my letters, it's very important I speak to you."

"So," he said slowly, like he was savoring the words. "Which of my girls did you know?"

This time, she wasn't able to stamp down the revulsion she felt. *His* girls. As if he owned them. As if by killing them, his victims belonged to him. Disgust curled inside her, and she had to stop her fists from curling too. She wanted nothing more than to get behind that Plexiglas and deck this bastard like the take-no-shit farm girl she was. But she had to confirm her suspicions. And that meant she had to stay calm.

She had to get him to make a mistake.

She wasn't stupid. He could pretend all he wanted, but he knew *exactly* who she was. He might've been in solitary, but a man like him? He had his ways. But she was going to let him draw his guessing game out. She wanted to know everything about how he viewed Cassie, how he talked about her, how he looked *when* he talked about her.

She was going to get to the bottom of this, even if it meant manipulating one of the most infamous serial killers of all time.

"You're what . . . early thirties?" he asked, openly assessing her now. "None of my girls had younger sisters who'd be that age now. So you . . . you must be a friend." His eyebrows raised in mock concern. "Did I take your best friend away from you?"

Abby didn't reply as she opened her notebook, flipping through the pages filled with her cramped handwriting. She did this deliberately slow, watching as he peered at the book, his interest evident.

Solitary drove most men to the brink. But this man? He wasn't even close to the edge.

He was bored. That's likely why he manipulated the other inmates—and apparently at least one guard—into killing themselves. It was a way to alleviate his boredom.

A bored serial killer was one who slipped up. Especially if she got him talking about the right things.

"Maybe a cousin?" he suggested, his mouth thinning at her silence. "A niece?"

Abby uncapped her pen, dropping it into the groove of her open notebook, and finally looked up to meet his eyes. And then she waited again. She counted silently to five, her pulse thundering in her ears as she refused to look away. Sweat trickled down between her shoulder blades, gathering at the small of her back.

Finally, when she had his complete attention, when it was just the two of them and his eyes drilled into hers, waiting for her to speak, she said: "Cassandra Martin." She enunciated each syllable with deadly weight. "You're going to tell me everything." She looked down at her watch. "You have twenty minutes."

CHAPTER 2

Sweat trickled down Paul's forehead as he bolted down the alleyway. The muggy DC air was so thick he could almost taste it as he moved, swift and silent, gun raised, eyes trained ahead, where the alley split off in two directions.

"We need him alive, Paul." It was Agent Grace Sinclair's voice in his ear. His profiler was back at headquarters. She'd sprained her ankle on their last case and still hadn't been cleared for field duty, a fact that made her use everything from espresso to chocolate chip cookies, trying to bribe him to clear her.

The problem with being friends with a profiler was that they honed in on all of a man's weaknesses. But Grace was no match for Paul when it came to the safety of his team. He wasn't going to let her out in the field injured, no matter how many cookies she baked.

Paul was almost to the fork in the alley, his pace slowing as his hand tightened around his Glock.

"You're going to want to take a right, boss." This time, it was Zooey, the team's tech and forensic expert, on the radio. "Security cameras show he ran into a dead end. He'll be heading back your way in twenty seconds."

"Got it," Paul said quietly. He moved to the right side of the alley, flattening himself against the brick wall as he moved swiftly toward the corner.

"Ten seconds," Zooey said.

Adrenaline pumped through him. A child had been taken from his mother. And he wasn't going to let either of them down.

"Five. Four. Three. Two. One."

A man in a tattered jean jacket bolted into the alley, looking around wildly.

"Harry Jordan!" Paul's voice boomed out, his gun trained on him.

The man jerked at his name, spinning around.

"Put the gun down," Paul warned, moving forward.

Harry stared at him, his face falling. "I didn't—" he started.

"Put the gun down, Harry," Paul said again. "Put it down and we can talk."

"Yeah, about what?" Harry asked. "You're just gonna shoot me." The gun in his hand wasn't raised. Paul had the upper hand here. And he needed to know where Harry had put the kid.

"I don't want to shoot you," Paul said. It was the truth. He wasn't that man. He'd taken lives before, necessary acts to protect others, but he knew the cost. "All I want is to bring Brandon home safe."

"Brandon is *my* son!" Harry shrieked, his voice going from quiet to screaming in just words.

"Paul, he's escalating," Grace said over the radio.

No shit, Paul thought.

"He is your son," Paul agreed. "But Haley is his mother and she has sole physical and legal custody. The courts decided that you need a year's worth of clean drug tests, before you're allowed to see him."

"It isn't fair!" Tears tracked down the man's face and Paul took advantage of his distraction to move forward.

"I know you're hurting," Paul said. "But this is where you prove that you're a good father, Harry. This is the moment where you put Brandon's needs before your own. And right now, Brandon needs to be safe at home with his mother. And you need to focus on getting clean."

Harry's face crumpled, like a building collapsing within itself. "I tried getting clean. I did. It's just . . . God, it's so hard. I just wanted to spend time with him. And then Haley said all those things in court—" More tears down his face. "They were true," he said. "God, they were all true."

"Careful, Paul," Grace warned. "We might not be looking at homicidal behavior here. This may turn into suicide or suicide-by-cop."

Paul's stomach clenched. Grace's read of the situation was right. Both his training and his gut were telling him so. He needed Harry to stay calm and to not panic or get too low.

He breathed in and out, wishing like hell that Grace was here to do this. Or Maggie Kincaid, the elite negotiator that worked on a case-by-case basis with his team. Both of them were better at this than him.

But right now, it was on him.

"You put the gun down and tell me where Brandon is, Harry, and I will personally talk to the DA about getting you in rehab. You can get clean. You can be a good father to your boy. You can start right now, by telling me where he is and putting that down. It's so easy. Simple. You want to be a good father, right?"

Harry nodded, but his grip on his gun was still tight. Paul eyed it, weighing his options.

"Then let's get started," Paul coaxed. "Where's Brandon?"

Harry's face crumpled, his shoulders slumping as all the fight seemed to drain out of him at once. "My buddy has a cabin outside of the city in Monkton. I took him there."

A flash of hope went through him—but he knew this was far from over. Just because Harry was handing over Brandon's location didn't mean he was going to come quietly—or at all.

"What's the address?" Paul asked.

"39821 Beaverton Road," Harry said.

"Got it, boss," Zooey said in his ear. "Agent Walker is in that area, questioning the grandparents. I'm sending the coordinates to him now."

"You're doing great," Paul told Harry, trying to sound as reassuring as possible. Harry still hadn't lowered his gun—it wasn't a good sign. "You're doing what's best for Brandon. Now it's time to do what's best for you."

Harry's hands went up and Paul tensed, the grip on his own gun tightening. But instead of pointing the gun at him, Harry clutched at his head with his free hand, tears coursing down his face as he placed the gun at his temple.

Grace's instincts and his own gut were right. This guy wasn't a murderer. He was suicidal.

Fuck. He felt horribly ill equipped for this. Usually when something like this happened, he had Grace at his side. As a psychologist, she had way better tools at handling a suicidal perp.

"No, Harry, don't do that," Paul said, his body going cold. "Don't do that to yourself. Don't do that to your kid."

"He's better off without me," Harry moaned.

"No, he's not," Paul said. "Don't do that to him. Don't make him grow up like that. You screwed up, Harry. You've made mistakes. But you've got a disease. And you can get help. You can recover."

"You don't know what it's like," Harry said, and Paul watched in horror as his finger shifted toward the trigger.

"I do, actually," he said.

The man's eyes, which had been unfocused and desperate, suddenly slid back to him. He had Harry's attention. Good. He was going to need it.

"First ten years of my life, my dad was black-out drunk for half of it, the other half, he was still drunk, but a happy drunk. Jovial. The life of the party. He was a funny guy when he was drinking. Everybody loved him. My mama loved him too." The gun was still on Harry's temple, but Paul could see his finger twitch away from the trigger, so it was resting on the barrel instead. Progress. Good.

"She had five children with him," he continued, taking a small step forward. "And the day he drove drunk and crashed his car? She kicked him to the curb that day and told him he wasn't allowed back until he got sober and stayed sober. So I think I know a little bit about this from your boy's perspective." Another step. Harry was watching him, transfixed, like Paul's voice was the only thing keeping him afloat.

"I know what it's like to have a shitty addict dad," Paul said, his confession quiet and somber. "But you know what, Harry? I also know what it's like to have a sober dad. One who coached my Little League team without the aid of a flask of whiskey, and who built a car with me when I was sixteen . . . the man who decided he loved his family more than he loved getting drunk. He made a choice. He confronted his disease. And he put in the work to get sober and to get his family back. When he passed a few years ago, he passed knowing that he'd done that work. He died sober and loved, surrounded by his children and friends and grandkids. That's the kind of life you want, Harry. That's the kind of death you want. You want to die when you're old, clean and sober and loved, and surrounded by people who care about you. You don't want this. You don't want Haley to have to explain to Brandon what happened to his dad. Don't take yourself from him. Decide right now to do the work. You put that gun down, Harry, and I will get you the help you need. I swear on my dad's grave."

Harry's large tormented eyes stared at him, the hope in them beautiful and terrible to behold.

"Just hand over the gun," Paul said. "Be the man you need to be for your son."

Harry's hand shook and then, *finally*, he lowered the gun.

It clattered to the ground and Harry fell to his knees, sobbing.

"Okay, Harry," Paul said, kicking the gun away and taking the cuffs out of his pocket. "I'm gonna do this gentle, okay?" He carefully restrained him, helping him to his feet once his hands were secure. "It's going to be all right," he assured him as Harry began to stumble down the alley next to him, still shaking with sobs.

"Boss, I just got word from Agent Walker that he has Brandon. He's fine. No trauma or awareness of the situation. He thought they were on a camping trip and that his mom knew all about it," Zooey said over the radio.

Paul felt a small sense of relief. Someday, Brandon would learn the truth. But at least for now, he could be unmarked by any trauma or worry. His mom would find a way to explain it to him when she thought it was appropriate.

"I've called Haley and she's on her way here to meet them," Grace added. "Good job, Paul. You defused the situation like a pro."

"We're heading in," Paul said.

"It's going to be okay," he told Harry again, as he opened the back of his SUV and shut it once Harry was safely inside.

Paul drove to headquarters, where Harry would be placed in custody.

He'd meant what he'd said—he'd work the system to get Harry the help he needed. But he also knew that with kidnapping charges laid against him, it was likely going to be a very long time—if ever—before Harry and Brandon were reunited.

It was always harder when the bad guy wasn't completely bad. When he was a victim of sorts as well. A victim of life, of abuse, of addiction. Paul had seen it all. It never got easier.

Never.

CHAPTER 3

A h, sweet Cass," Howard said, a smile flitting across his thin lips.

A shiver went through Abby, a reaction to the smile on his face that she couldn't stop. It wasn't a malicious smile, or one of perverse pleasure.

No, this was a smile of *fondness*. Of *affection*. Like he was a normal man thinking of a grandchild.

Abby swallowed, her throat suddenly and terribly dry. She didn't want to show weakness—a croaky throat or a cracked voice would delight him to no end.

"Let me guess," he said. "You're doing a story on Dr. X's last victim. What's your angle, Lois Lane? You've got to have something fresh."

"Let's start with August of 2000," Abby said, flipping through her notebook to where her time line was scrawled.

"Why in the world would we start there?" he asked. "That's a full three years before I found sweet little Cassandra and made her mine."

You cannot try to stab this guy with a pen, no matter how much you want to, she thought as her grip slipped on the pen in question. It was a miracle the guards had even let her in with one—she'd been prepared to bring her tablet to take notes—but she guessed that with Howard in a straitjacket, they felt it wasn't as much of a security risk.

"I want to start in August of 2000," Abby repeated, like a preschool teacher would say to a toddler. Annoyance flared in his eyes, and she felt a small burst of pleasure. Good. She was getting to him.

"What about August of 2000?" he demanded, his shoulders tensing underneath the rough canvas of the jacket.

"You were in Medford, Oregon, during that time, working as a coroner, is that correct?"

"Yes."

"And five years before that, in 1995, you retired as chief of surgery from a hospital in Los Angeles?" Abby asked.

"Clearly you have the information that confirms that in front of you, Ms. Winthrop," he said.

"I always like to check my facts with the original source," she said, and even though it killed her, she let a corner of her mouth quirk up a bit, a fleeting hint of a smile that would fuel him. "You know, there's a theory that you left surgery and became a coroner because you were trying to resist your urge to kill."

He chuckled, a grating sound that was all egotistical pleasure. "Is that what you think?"

"I don't think you've ever resisted an urge in your life," Abby said. "I think you like power, in any form. I think you *really* like cutting people up, but you prefer they're sweet little brunettes and you prefer them dead by your hands. I think there's probably dozens of cardio patients you treated who fit that type who never got off your operating table and at least a half a dozen dead girls' names and locations you've never turned over to the FBI."

"I see we're finally expressing ourselves," he said. "I like this side of you, Abigail. This isn't just a story for you, is it? You're not just a journalist chasing down a lead. You're *dogged*. Unhealthily obsessed, some might say. I was right before: This is personal. You knew Cassandra Martin." His head tilted as he took her in for a second time, armed with this information. "That means you must be from around Castella

Rock," he said. "I thought I smelled the barn on you. Oh, farm girls." He shook his head. "So stubborn. They need to be broken like horses. I never saw the point of exerting that much effort. I like my girls sweet and easy. That's why I chose Cassie."

Abby gritted her teeth against the retort she wanted to throw at him. She hated that he called her Cassie—God, no one ever called her that— and talked about her like he knew her. Like he was entitled to a nickname. Screw him. He wasn't entitled to any part of her.

"Do you want to know what did it for me?" He leaned forward conspiratorially. "Those curls. Ringlets like a porcelain doll. The second I saw them, I just knew I had to get my hands wrapped around them."

And there it was. Triumph soared through her as that horrible, gnawing gut feeling she'd had since she started this was finally confirmed.

Cass hadn't worn her hair in curls since their freshman year of high school. She started straightening it every morning, a rebellious move against her mother, who had used to put her in those child beauty pageants and had loved her curls. And her hair certainly hadn't been curly that night she was taken. Abby knew that personally.

No, the only time her hair had been curly that year was for her yearbook photos. She'd done it on the condition that her mother would pay for a professional photographer. *Sometimes I've got to throw her a bone, Abby*, she remembered Cass telling her.

"What are you doing?" Howard demanded, his eyes fixed on the now-closed notebook.

"We're done here," Abby said.

His gray eyebrows drew together. "You spent all this time trying to see me, and you're leaving after two questions."

"I don't need you to answer any more questions," Abby said. "You've told me everything I need to know."

His frown deepened, his lips curling in distaste. This wasn't going how he pictured it. He wasn't in control anymore.

He didn't understand he'd just made the mistake she'd been waiting for.

"You asked me what my angle was," Abby said, staring him down, her eyes hard and piercing. "You really want to know?" She got to her feet, stepping forward, until she was just inches from the Plexiglas. She was so close she could see his quick, excited intake of breath at her proximity and the flutter of his nostrils as he breathed her in.

"You didn't kill her," Abby said. "You weren't even there that night. I don't think you even knew Cassandra Martin's name until the sheriff busted down the door of your RV and brought you in for questioning."

Howard Wells was a lot of things—a sociopath, a sadist, an unrepentant, gleeful murderer—but even he couldn't control his body's reactions. Abby watched with satisfaction as the blood drained out of the man's face.

"I figured it out, Howard," she said, her voice lowering. "You were playing a game. But you can't play a game with just one person. You had a friend. Or as close to a friend as someone like you two can get. Someone who was like you. A kindred twisted spirit. What happened? Did you think you had a teammate when he was really an opponent?"

"Quiet," he ground out. Sweat popped along his forehead, a bead trickling down his temple.

"He got the better of you," Abby said. "Your little friend set you up. He was smarter than you and you were stupid enough to walk into his trap. Is that why you claimed Cass? Because he *humiliated* you by being more clever than you?"

He lunged for her, slamming his shoulder against the window.

Instead of flinching or shrinking away, Abby slapped her palm on the glass herself, standing tall and strong, lip curling. He didn't startle, but his eyes widened at her reaction.

"I'm coming for your playmate, Wells," she snarled. "Both of you are just predators, circling the flock. And you know what farm girls like me have been taught to do to predators?" She tilted her chin up, ever her father's stubborn, solid girl, facing down a man who'd killed more people than she had fingers. "We shoot 'em dead."

His eyes nearly bugged out of his head at her words and he slammed his torso against the window, screaming, spittle and blood flying from his mouth, babbling threat after threat as the guard came racing inside.

"Ms. Winthrop!" he said, tugging at her arm. "You need to get out of here."

But Abby stood where she was, just for one more moment, standing tall.

She had been right. Her knees felt shaky with relief as she let Stan steer her away.

This was far from over.

She was just getting started.

CHAPTER 4

By the time Harry was processed and in police custody, it was late. Paul loosened his tie, tugging it off as he sat down in his leather chair. His office was quiet—most of the floor had gone home by this time. A relatively silent night—if there really ever was one when you worked for the FBI.

His eyes felt gritty—he couldn't remember the last time he slept. They'd gotten the call about Brandon two . . . was it three days ago? Haley Ellis was a senator's chief of staff, and their team had been called in as a special favor.

He was just glad it had worked out as seamlessly as it did. Usually kidnapping cases—even in the cases of one parent kidnapping the child—ended badly. Especially after a certain amount of time had passed.

There was a light knock on the door, and a woman with long, dark hair peeked her head in.

He waved her in. "Hey, Grace."

She set a cup of espresso on his desk with a smile.

He shot her a look. "I'm still not clearing you without a doctor's note," he said.

She rolled her eyes. "I'm not trying to bribe you. I'm trying to be nice. You did a really good job out there today."

He took a gulp of the bracing drink, feeling better with each swallow. "I'm really relieved it worked out the way it did."

"It worked out that way because of you," Grace said. "I couldn't have done any better."

This time, he was rolling his eyes. He had the privilege of working with some incredibly gifted and strong women—something his childhood growing up with four sisters had certainly prepared him for.

Grace was the definition of *brilliant*: an accomplished psychologist and profiler—and a bestselling author on top of that. Her insight and intellect were extraordinary.

He wasn't egotistical enough—or delusional enough—to think he was even close to her level when it came to brains. He was a damn good FBI agent—and he hoped an even better team leader. He strived to be a good man—in his life and his work. But he was straightforward; someone who looked at situations from as many angles as he could before making his decisions. He liked rules and the methodology of solving crimes, finding each piece and examining it with careful precision and putting each piece together to see the greater picture. It was often the slower way of catching criminals, but it served him—and the country he loved—well.

"Are you going home before your flight?" Grace asked.

Paul shook his head. He was flying back to California tomorrow—or, technically, it was today, he thought as he glanced at the clock on his desk. "I need to be at the airport in three hours. I'll just finish up my paperwork here and then go. I've got my luggage in the car."

"Are you excited to see your family?" she asked.

"It's always good to go back home," he said, and he knew she heard the noncommittal tone in his voice because even *he* could hear it.

He winced mentally. He tried hard not to be on edge around Grace. She was a truly loyal friend, an amazing FBI agent, and a vital addition to his team. But what made her so important to the team also gave her the ability to see through people like they were glass. She had an agreement with the team that she wouldn't profile them . . . at least to their faces. But sometimes that extraordinary brain of hers just couldn't stop turning and ferreting out truths.

He waited for her to say something about his confession to Harry. He wondered briefly if she had figured this out about him already—that he had an alcoholic father. It was likely, he thought with resigned humor. She'd probably respected his privacy too much to mention it.

Sometimes, he let himself wonder if she'd figured out the *real* truth. The one that had shaped him. That had put him on this path.

He didn't share that with anyone. Not even Maggie, the woman he'd planned on marrying before her own past had torn them apart. He had loved Maggie, but he hadn't been able to share the dark piece of his past that had formed his whole future—his whole self.

As his trip back home loomed closer, he had been thinking about it a lot lately. He'd been thinking about *her*. Cass. It was still hard to even think her name, let alone speak it, even though it had been fifteen years now.

". . . need another?"

"What?" Paul jerked out of his reverie to find Grace's eyebrows knit together as she stared at him with concern.

"An espresso. Do you need another?" she repeated. "Seems like you do. Are you sure you're okay to drive to the airport? I can call you a car. Or drive you myself."

"I'm fine," he assured her. "I don't need more coffee. I'm just thinking about going home. It's been a few years."

Grace's face shifted from concern to sympathy. "Of course," she said. "I understand. I'm sure your father's memorial brings up a lot of stuff."

He nodded. It was a half-truth. His father had been gone for five years now, and every year, the Harrison clan gathered on his birthday at the orchard house that had been in their family for generations, to pay tribute. He had missed the last two years because of cases—something his family understood—but he had heard the hopeful note in his mother's voice when she'd called about this year. And he'd been determined to go, for her.

"I'll let you get to your paperwork," Grace said, getting to her feet and heading to the door.

"Try not to let Zooey burn the place down while I'm gone," he said.

"That was one time!" Grace protested. "It was a *tiny* fire that was quickly contained. And I wasn't even in charge while you were at that conference. Gavin was!"

He laughed. "That's why I put *you* in charge this time," he said.

Grace smiled smugly in response. "Have a good time with your family."

"I will. And thank you for taking the helm while I'm gone."

"All in a day's work," Grace said. "Have a safe flight."

Once he was alone again, he turned back to his paperwork. This time, he was unable to push his thoughts of home—and of the past, away.

The Cass in his mind was beautiful and bright, an eternal seventeen, a tangle of brown hair, sweet words, and fuzzy laughter he couldn't quite remember right. She was also a white marble headstone, the tears down Mrs. Martin's face, and *why weren't you with her that night, Paul?*

He sighed, his heart aching in his chest as he thought of home, of the rows of almond and olive trees for as far as the eye could see, and of a girl who was taken much too soon and who had shaped his life without ever knowing it.

CHAPTER 5

Abby got back to the farmhouse late—it was nearly 2:00 a.m. before she pulled her battered Chevy truck in front of the fading rust-red barn, its tin roof glinting in the beam of the headlights.

The house was quiet when she let herself in. Roscoe, the ancient Great Pyrenees who'd grown up guarding the goat flock that used to live in the north field, barked once, but upon seeing her, started wagging his tail instead.

"Hey, boy," she said, scratching his ears. He was a big white beast that looked like he had more in common with a polar bear than a dog.

Roscoe was much too old to guard any livestock now. These days he spent his time dozing in whatever doorway he deemed vital to guard that day. He was a sweet-natured boy who still wandered out to the north field from time to time, looking confused, like he was wondering where his herd went.

When her father had been diagnosed with colon cancer, she had sold the goats, unable to take care of an entire herd *and* the orchard and her father. Sometimes she thought about getting a new herd—her orchard manager had been making noises about wanting goats to help clear some of the neglected meadows. It would surely cheer Roscoe.

She knew she should sleep, but the years of being an insomniac added to the years of nursing her father, and she had some hardwired night-owl habits. Plus, her mind was still working a mile a minute, going over every second of her meeting with Wells.

She'd thought of nothing else on the long drive back home. She prided herself on the fact that she had to pull over to throw up only once, dizzy from the adrenaline, the fear, the sick realization that Cass's *real* killer was still loose, that he'd been free and out there walking around this whole time, churning hot in her stomach.

She checked Roscoe's water bowl and food, as well as the corkboard in the mudroom where her staff left her notes when they couldn't reach her on the phone. After toeing off her shoes and shoving her feet into her rubber boots, she was almost ready.

"You want to go for a nighttime walk, boy?" she asked Roscoe, who wagged his tail enthusiastically at the word *walk*.

On her way out of the house, she grabbed one of her grandmother's crocheted shawls and wrapped it around her shoulders. With a lantern in one hand and Roscoe's leash in the other, they ventured out into the night.

THE WINTHROP ORCHARD was 150 acres of almond trees, fifty acres of olive trees, and ten acres of grapes that never quite made good wine, so they made small batches of good vinegar from the grape must. These 210 acres were her family history. Generations of Winthrops had put their blood, sweat, and tears into this place.

In her youth, this place had felt like a cage. She'd been desperate to leave Castella Rock, to explore other places, to meet other people. She'd felt stifled by the expectations of her father— he'd wanted her to stay. And maybe, if things had been different, she would have.

But Cass . . . her death changed everything.

Abby opened the orchard gate, letting Roscoe go first, tugging at his leash as she closed the gate behind them. The trees spread in neat rows ahead of her, lines and lines of old trees, good trees.

There are strong roots here, Abby, her father used to say to her. *Your roots.*

When she was a child, she used to play hide-and-seek between the rows of trees. When she was a teenager, she used to go out here with boys. She remembered letting herself be pressed against the trunk by eager but inexperienced hands, laughing giddily against a clumsy but eager mouth, not quite in love, but near it and everything so new and marvelous.

The shadows of the trees—their leaves lush and their branches heavy with nuts—stretched across her body as she plunged into the embrace of the orchard, the sky disappearing underneath the canopy of leaves, coolness slipping over her as she breathed in the scent of coming rain and freshly turned earth.

As she moved deeper into the trees, into the safe hold of the roots and branches that had sheltered her throughout her life, she let her mind return to Cass. And to Howard Wells.

When she moved back home, she hadn't even thought about writing a book about Cass. She'd been focused on getting her dad healthy . . . but that didn't happen. And then she found herself dealing with his terminal cancer and an orchard that needed to be nursed back to life, and by the time she looked up again, able to breathe, years had passed. And she needed a change.

She didn't want to just write investigative pieces for magazines and websites anymore. She wanted to do something bigger. Something personal. And when Cass's mother asked her to write about her daughter, she couldn't say no. So Abby set out to write a book about Cass's life—and her loss. A tale of a town in mourning . . . and then a town haunted, by the specter of a man too terrible to comprehend and the last girl he ever killed.

She hadn't wanted to be focused on Wells—there were plenty of books about the methodology—and psychology—of Dr. X. She wasn't a psychologist, she wasn't interested in profiling him or dedicating more ink and paper and words to his evil. When it came to killers like him, the ones that were so horrible, so vile, so profane against the very humanity they came from, their victims always got lost in the shuffle.

She was interested in telling Cass's story.

But as she began to research it, Cass's story took a turn. It started when she got her hands on the police interviews with Wells and compared them to the FBI tapes. It had taken a lot of favors to get both—the FBI had taken over the case pretty fast—but their local police had done the initial arrest and questioning. When she compared the police interviews with those conducted by the FBI, the first inkling that something wasn't quite right began to snake its way into her mind.

"Abby?"

A voice jerked her out of her thoughts, and Roscoe barked, tugging on his leash.

She was sure she was dreaming as the figure broke through the fog and she got a clear view of him.

It was him. Standing there like the answer to all the questions she'd been asking herself. For a moment, she just stared at him, her mouth hanging open. And then she snapped her jaw shut and said, "Paul."

Roscoe was still pulling on his leash, so Abby snapped her fingers. "Settle, boy."

Paul's handsome face broke out into a smile—so familiar, but different at the same time. His eyes crinkled in places they didn't before, but his hair was still that unruly shock of gold, dipping into his bright blue eyes.

"I'm sorry, I didn't mean to scare you."

He held out his arms and she stepped forward into them, letting him hug her. He smelled like the orchard, like green fresh leaves and summer, of memories she'd tried to avoid and promises she'd broken.

She closed her eyes, breathing it all in, trying to calm her thundering heart.

It was hammering harder in her chest now than it had been at the prison. Yet she had nothing to fear from Paul.

Except her own damn weakness.

"It's good to see you," he said when they pulled apart. "What are you doing wandering the rows this late?"

"It's my orchard," she said, feeling that telltale defensive prickle up her spine. "I can walk it in the middle of the night if I want."

His smile grew wider. "Same old Abby," he said.

She folded her arms across her chest. Now that Roscoe knew he was a friend, the old dog had sat at her feet, his tongue lolling out of his mouth to an impressive length. "It's been a long time," she said pointedly.

Three years. She remembered all too well the last time they'd been face-to-face. It hadn't ended pleasantly.

Paul's mother, when Abby saw her every weekend at the farmer's market, liked to complain about how her son never visited. Tandy

Harrison was a battle-axe of a woman, if you ever met one. She wasn't ever a farmer's wife—she was a farmer herself, first and foremost.

For all of Abby's life, the Harrisons had been their next-door neighbors—well, as close to next door as you could get with acres of land between their houses. Tandy had spearheaded a weekly rotation among her father's old friends to sit with him once a week, giving Abby some free time to herself. Tandy was the type who looked out for her own—and she pretty much considered the entire population of Castella Rock her own.

Abby was grateful to her and admired her. When she was younger, Tandy was the closest thing to a mother figure she had. And now that she was a grown woman, she was the valued giver of insight that Abby sought when it came to all things regarding the orchard.

"I'm home for the memorial," Paul said. "Will you be there?"

Abby nodded. "Of course."

They looked at each other, the silence stretching between them.

It shouldn't be this awkward. She'd known him her entire life. He was the boy next door. She'd crossed the meadow between their properties thousands of times, looking for him. He'd been her first kiss, when she was six. And she'd "married" him when they were seven, with ring-pops they'd stolen from one of his sisters.

He was woven into the tapestry of her life and stories. When he and Cass had gotten together, it had made sense. They fit together. And Abby was happy that the two people closest to her loved each other.

But by the time they were seventeen, things had changed. They all had changed.

Except for Cass. Cass hadn't lived long enough to change.

Her stomach twisted at the long-buried thought. "I should get back," she said, jerking her thumb behind her. "It's late."

He nodded, shoving his hands in his pockets, and for a second, he looked so much like the boy she knew, it took her breath away. "I . . ."

Oh, God. Please don't let him bring it up, she thought. *Please let him just let it lie.*

The last time they'd seen each other, it had been a disaster. She'd been grieving. They'd both been drinking. It had gotten terribly, terribly messy. And they hadn't spoken since then. He hadn't come home since then. She hated the idea that maybe she was the reason he stayed away.

"It's good to see you," he said. "I'm glad you're coming tomorrow."

"I wouldn't miss it," she said, and then mentally winced, because she knew he *had* missed it the past few years. She'd worried, that first year, if it was because of her. But Tandy had told her he had a case. She prayed that was the truth. She hated the idea of what happened between them keeping him from his family and their traditions.

"Then I guess I'll see you there."

"Yeah."

She turned to go, and as she was walking away, she heard him say, "Night, Winny," and the sound of her childhood nickname, the one only he and Cass called her, made unexpected tears prick the corners of her eyes.

She took a deep breath, tightening her hands on Roscoe's leash, and continued through the rows of trees, leaving Paul behind.

It was what she was good at, after all.

CHAPTER 6

Two years ago

The funeral had been beautiful. Abby had made sure of that. She felt an ache down to her very bones as she dragged herself up the porch steps of the farmhouse. She'd spent the last week and a half frantically running around, arranging everything, getting the service ready, the flowers, the programs, all the food.

And now, it was finally over.

Now, she could finally grieve. Alone. Away from the well-wishers and the concerned neighbors and everyone from church who just wanted to help.

She just needed to get inside the house and lie down.

"Hey, Winny."

The voice, soft, rough, and so familiar, sent a warm rush of relief through her.

He'd come.

She turned, and Paul was standing there at the bottom of the porch steps, looking like he'd just gotten off a plane. His hair was rumpled, and his wrinkled shirt was open at the collar.

"I'm so sorry I wasn't able to make it for the service," he said.

"I'm just glad you're here," she answered. "Come on in."

They settled in her kitchen with a bottle of whiskey, and it was just like old times. They toasted her father, to the good memories, but with each drink, the bad ones began to come out.

"How's work?" she asked, as they moved into the living room, sitting next to each other on the couch. She tossed her legs over his lap and he tugged at the little anklet—a string of stars—she had on, grinning.

"Cute," he said.

"Be nice. Your niece gave me that," she said.

"Which one?" he asked.

"Robin," she answered. "She's a sweetie. Very laid back."

"You sound surprised," he said.

"Well, she is Georgia's kid," Abby said, and he found this hilarious, laughing so long and hard that Abby found her eyes lingering on his lips, on the way his blue eyes crinkled at the edges. She could feel something stirring inside her—something that had nothing to do with the whiskey.

Something that would only be quelled with *more* whiskey. Because the other option?

The other option was swinging her legs on either side of him, straddling his lap and taking his face in her hands and kissing him.

It wasn't like she hadn't thought about it. Right now it was all she could think about.

It wasn't like she didn't know what it felt like, kissing him.

That other time, when they had been teenagers, had been fueled by grief too. By tears and by loss and by the two of them, too young and too desperate for some reprieve.

It would be like that now too.

You're grieving, Abby, she told herself. *Stop being weak. Dad wouldn't want you to be.*

Who the hell knew what her father really had wanted. He had loved her, she supposed, in his own way. But he'd never intended to be raising a daughter alone. Losing her mother had been an emotional blow the two of them had never managed to navigate.

And now they never would.

She knocked back another shot, trying to shut out the want and the grief and the pain. How many was that, now?

Did it matter? Her father was dead and Cass was dead, and now it was just her. And Paul, when he had the time to show up.

"Do you ever think about her?" she asked, suddenly, compelled to bring her up. Because if she brought Cass up, she wouldn't have to think about the man next to her, how good he was, how right he felt, how his smile lit her up inside like Christmas.

How many times had she put Cass's ghost between them? She'd lost count. It was such a convenient barrier against her true feelings.

You're such a martyr. She could practically *hear* Cass's voice in her head. She had clearly had too much to drink. She set the whiskey bottle on the wagon wheel coffee table and leaned against the couch.

"Sometimes," he said, and she realized he was answering her question. "On her birthday, usually. I like to call Mrs. Martin and check in on her."

"That's nice of you," Abby said.

"I don't know about that," Paul said. "Sometimes I think it's more guilt than anything."

"You have nothing to feel guilty about," Abby said.

She, on the other hand . . .

Don't think about that.

"I miss her," she said softly. "I wonder about who she would've been."

He was quiet. She wondered if he let himself ponder the same things. Or if it was just too damn painful.

"She would've been proud of you," Paul said.

Abby tried to arch an eyebrow, but she had a feeling she looked funny, because his eyes were twinkling at her.

"With how much she teased me about joining the school newspaper freshman year?" She laughed.

"She was jealous," Paul said. "She even told me so, when I pointed out she was kind of being a jerk."

She could feel her mouth twisting, trying not to smile at this revelation. "Is that why she apologized to me? She baked me an apology pie and everything."

"Well, I didn't tell her to bake a pie," Paul said. "But yeah, I told her she was being mean. She *was* being mean. She was afraid you were going to go off with the smart kids and leave her behind."

"I would've never," Abby whispered fiercely, her heart heavy that Cass ever even thought that for a minute. It was still hard to accept that near the end, Cass had thought a lot worse of her.

"I know," Paul said quietly. "And she knew, deep down. She was just scared of losing you. She knew you'd go off to college someday and she . . ."

"She wanted to stay," Abby finished. Cass had always wanted to stay in Castella Rock. She had never been that small-town girl who harbored bigger dreams of the city. To her, all those big dreams were right there at home. "But then she never got to leave."

"Hey." He shifted in his seat so he was facing her, and he cupped her cheek, brushing away the unexpected tear. "I'm sorry," he said. "We shouldn't talk about heavy stuff. Not after today."

Because she'd buried her father today. God, she was exhausted. She let out a shuddery little breath, the realization hitting her as the warmth of his skin spread against hers.

It felt so good, his skin on hers. Like the memory of something she'd lost a long time ago. His hand came up, almost as if it had a mind of its own, covering hers.

Her eyes met his, and her heart flipped over in her chest, a rush of *yes* coming over her as his thumb stroked down her neck and he murmured her name.

The kiss was feather-soft. Almost a suggestion, full of hesitation, of tightly restrained desire. And then her mouth opened underneath his, a surge of heat and *finally* rushing through her, blotting out everything else, just for a moment.

For a moment, it was the two of them and nothing else existed. It was his hands in her hair and his lips moving against hers and his taste—spice and whiskey—on her tongue.

For a moment, there was no history, no past, no future. Just then.

Just *them*.

But when that moment shattered, she remembered.

Cass.

She jerked back, pushing herself away, off the couch entirely, trying to ignore how even as she was retreating, he was reaching for her.

"You're drunk. I'm drunk. We . . . this isn't right," she said, trembling, trying not to feel like there was a hole forming inside her. Like the memory of his lips against hers wasn't going to haunt her till the day she died.

"Abby," he said, a slow rumble of sound that shot through her like a bullet.

"Don't," she begged. "Don't let me dishonor her memory. Please don't do that to me."

"Wait—" Paul said, but she had whirled around, hurrying upstairs, her heart aching for so many reasons.

The next morning, she woke hungover as hell.

When she went downstairs, the living room was empty. But there was a note on the wagon wheel coffee table.

All it said was: *I'm sorry.*

CHAPTER 7

Paul looked out across the meadow that separated his family's orchard from Abby's. The rows of picnic tables had been set up in the center of the meadow, lupine and California poppies speckling the tall grasses. There were big tin tubs of ice set all over, full of bottles of specialty old-fashioned homemade sodas—his father's hobby after he had quit drinking, and one his sister Faye had picked up. A huge BBQ pit had been set up, the coals already layered with a fine coat of ash as the tri-tip and chicken sizzled above them.

It had been a beautiful memorial. They'd risen early and gone out to the hill at the very back of the property, where a simple wooden cross lay. His father's ashes were in an urn on the mantel, but the hill, his father's favorite place, was sacred to his mother. He knew she went there often to feel closer to him, and it was fitting that each year they gathered at the hill, to speak their piece and their hearts about the man who'd helped shape them.

And now it was time to celebrate him in the style he would have loved, with good music, good food, and good friends.

"Uncle Paul!" Robin, his oldest niece from his sister Georgia's family, bounded up to him and hugged him. "I'm so glad you came."

He hugged her back. "Me too," he said, and he did mean it, even though this day had been difficult.

"Come sit with me!" Robin tugged on his arm, heading toward the picnic tables. "I want to talk to you."

He followed her, the two of them taking a spot at the end of one of the tables, away from most of the crowd. The smell of barbecue was heavy in the air, and the music and talk floated along the meadow.

His father would have loved this. Laughter. Family. Food. Friends. A celebration of life, of his memory, instead of something somber. He looked over to his mother and smiled, thinking how lucky his dad had been—how lucky his entire family was, to have such a strong and gracious woman as the head of their family.

"So, how's school?" he asked Robin, grabbing

a chip from one of the bowls on the table and dipping it in his sister Faye's famous nectarine salsa. It was just like he remembered: tart, fruity, with a slow burn of heat. He used to joke that Faye should jar the stuff and sell it—and she had taken him seriously. Now Aunt Faye's salsa—along with other specialty condiments and the entire soda line—was for sale all over the West Coast in only the finest grocery stores. A few months ago, both Costco and Trader Joe's had reached out. Expanding had been a lot of work, but Faye thrived in stressful environments. Before she'd become a salsa and soda maven, she'd been an EMT. She still worked for the volunteer fire department in town.

"It's great," Robin said. "I got all the AP classes I wanted and I successfully lobbied the school board to let me join the wrestling team."

"I heard about that," Paul said. He'd been incredibly impressed with Robin, who, when she signed up for wrestling tryouts, had been rejected by the coach because she was a girl. Considering Robin had been taking mixed martial arts classes since she was a kid, it was a hard blow for her. But not one to be discouraged—she was a lot like her grandmother in that way— she'd taken her fight to the principal and then the school board—and won.

She'd also won three of her first six matches. Turned out she had a real talent for multiple fighting arts.

"The guys on the team aren't giving you a hard time, are they?" he asked, concerned.

Robin shook her head. "We're cool," she said. "A lot of them are in my MMA classes. *They* respect me. Coach is the only one who thinks I'm weird."

"You're not weird," Paul said firmly, wondering if he had time to swing by the school and have a little talk with Coach Patten. He remembered the guy from *his* school days. He was a hard-ass who was just getting his start in coaching back then and clearly still had that misogynistic streak that made him complain mightily to the baseball team about being forced to coach the girls' softball team. "And if Coach Patten gives you any shit, you call me."

"Uncle Paul!" She laughed at his swearing, and he laughed too. Georgia, her mother, *hated* cursing. His oldest sister was an absolute sweetie, but she was a little traditional and prim. So, naturally, she ended up with a five-foot-ten daughter with wild hair and a wilder spirit.

She's got more of Jason than me in her, his sister would say with a smile. *And that makes me love her even more.*

"I'm really glad you're enjoying school," he said. "Your mom start in on you about college yet?"

"That's actually kind of what I wanted to talk to you about," Robin said.

"Oh?" he asked. "Are you looking at some colleges in DC or back east? Because I'd love to show you around if you want to tour them."

"It's not that," Robin said. "Though I'd totally love to do that. It's . . ." She looked over her shoulder, scanning the crowd, and Paul realized she was making sure her mom was out of earshot. His curiosity piqued, he leaned forward.

"I wanted to talk to you. About the FBI."

"What about it?"

"I know I need a degree before I'm even considered for Quantico," Robin said. "And I know I have to be twenty-three. But I was curious if there were, like, degrees or schools that would be better for me if the FBI was my end goal."

Paul's throat felt tight with emotion. "You want to join the FBI?" he asked. If she knew the requirements she needed to get into Quantico, she'd obviously done some research on this.

"Yes," Robin said. "I want to help people. Serve my country. I want to be like you, Uncle Paul."

His heart suddenly felt too big for his body, pride rising inside him.

"Do you . . . do you think they'd want me?" Robin asked, a flash of insecurity playing across her round, freckled face.

"Yes," Paul said. "You are exactly the kind of young woman that the FBI would want. You're smart, you're capable, you think on your feet, and if your mother's bragging isn't exaggerated, you have a real gift for languages."

"I'm taking Spanish and French 4 this year," Robin said. "And I'm learning Mandarin on the side. Dad found me an online class. We've been taking it together."

"Those are all big assets in the FBI," Paul said. "And the fact that you're very physically fit and know how to take care of yourself? Also big plusses. We would need to work on your marksmanship, though."

"We?" she asked.

"If you want, you can come stay with me next summer for a while. I won't be able to take you on cases, of course, but we can go to the firing range, you can meet my team, tour Quantico, tour the headquarters, get a feel for the place. See if it's a good fit. I think it will be."

Robin's mouth twisted, unsure. "You think Mom would let me?"

Oh. There was that. Georgia wasn't exactly a helicopter mom, but Robin was her only child. His big sister had dealt with infertility and then a very difficult birth, and she and Jason hadn't been able to have more kids. They'd poured their energy into Robin and their extended family. And Robin had cousins her age, which was like having a sibling when you were a Harrison.

Paul was the only one who'd left California. At least, until Robin flew the nest in two years. She was the oldest grandchild, and he knew that it would make Georgia and his mother simultaneously proud and terrified if Robin decided to pursue the FBI as a career.

"I will talk to her," Paul said.

"She doesn't know. About the whole FBI thing," Robin explained. "I think she might freak out a little. She worries about you a *lot*."

"Your mom is a worrier," Paul said, with a smile. "But she does have reason to worry. My job's not always a safe one."

He hadn't told his family about the events nearly a year ago, when he'd made a terrible call and paid the price. Three nights out of seven, he still woke up in a cold sweat, the weight of that bomb vest a phantom memory against his skin. It used to be every night, so he figured he was making some progress. After Grace had confronted him about his PTSD during a difficult case where he kept pulling her back in fear of one of his team getting hurt, he'd made himself return to therapy.

"But the job's worth it, isn't it?" Robin asked earnestly. "You wouldn't do it if it wasn't."

"It's worth it," Paul said, trying not to think of that weight pressing on his chest.

"What are you two talking about?"

His mother came to sit next to him, putting her arm around him.

"Oh, just thinking maybe Robin might come visit me in DC next summer," Paul said. "Check out some of the colleges on the East Coast. We gotta ask Georgia and Jason first, though."

"That's a wonderful idea," his mom said. "Dear, we're almost out of the homemade sarsaparilla. Abby was a sweetie, she's storing all the extra beverages at her place because it's closer. Will you go get us a few crates? The dolly's over there."

"Sure," Paul said, getting to his feet. He needed to walk off all the barbecue he'd eaten anyway. And he couldn't help but crave a few moments of silence to himself. He loved his family, loved the hustle and bustle of it, but he'd been gone a long time, and it was sometimes hard to adjust. "Be back in a while."

"Thanks, sweetie," his mom called, losing herself in a conversation with Robin about her upcoming wrestling meet.

Paul snagged the dolly, stopping to greet Gray Teller, one of his old teammates from baseball, before heading out across the meadow. The music and noise faded as he walked farther away from the party, and he made his way down the winding path that led to Abby's house, thinking he could walk this road with his eyes closed.

He'd certainly walked it enough drunk when he was a teen, he thought with a wry grin.

The Winthrop farmhouse was just as he remembered it—a slice out of time—the red shutters gleaming against the white two-story edifice. The double wraparound porch rails were painted a shiny black that gleamed under the porch light, and the old oak tree in the front yard—the one he'd learned to climb on—still had the tire swing roped to the biggest branch.

Abby and her giant beast of a dog were still at the party, so he didn't knock, but just let himself in. It felt a little strange walking through Abby's house without her permission, but technically, his mom had permission. And she sent him.

Inside, the house was the same as he remembered, but also different. There were flashes of modern touches amongst the 1930s farmhouse decor—a gray suede couch had replaced the ancient brown one he remembered, a deep purple chenille throw tossed over it, a book lying on the wagon wheel coffee table that he *did* remember. He glanced at the cover, amused when he saw it was Grace's latest book. Maybe he'd get her to sign a copy for Abby, send it to her as a way to mend what was broken between them.

God, he hated where the two of them were. Seeing her in the orchard last night—and at the memorial today—had just brought it all back.

The last time he saw Abby, when her father had died, he had fucked things up royally. And he'd never apologized. He'd run, like a coward. He didn't have any excuses. It had been a shitty thing to do. The fight they'd had . . .

He'd lost a piece of himself when he left her. The piece of him that she'd always held in her hand, the fiery girl across the meadow who was in half of his childhood memories and almost all of his teenage ones. She was a permanent fixture in his life that he'd spent the last few years ignoring because he hadn't been big enough to say *I'm sorry.*

He needed to make it right before he left, he decided as he headed into the kitchen to search for the crates of soda. He couldn't find them, so he headed to the mudroom, thinking they might be there. But   ty, with just Abby's bright yel.   boots and Roscoe's hair-covered do.,   began to search the downstairs for the soda, opening each door as he went. When he reached the study, he glanced inside. The room was dark, the blinds pulled. He searched along the wall for the light switch, flipping it on.

As soon as the light filled the room, he wished he hadn't.

There were four whiteboards set along the far wall of the study, one labeled CASS, the second labeled X, the third with a question mark, and the fourth . . .

The fourth just said EVIDENCE.

Paul stepped farther into the room, his mouth going dry as his eyes fell on Cass's whiteboard. On the picture of her there.

God. He hadn't looked at the photos he had stashed away in years. He'd left himself with just his memories of her.

He'd forgotten how bright her smile was. How her dimple used to flash at him when she teased him.

His eyes tracked lower, to a piece of paper affixed to the board. His frown deepened as he read the paper, scribbled in what he recognized as Abby's cramped handwriting:

1:30 PM: C calls to cancel
2:00 PM: C leaves house
2:30 PM: C arrives at Physical Therapy
4:00 PM: C leaves Physical Therapy
4–7: ???? Unknown
7:00–7:40: Unsub takes Cass

His eyes snagged on the last entry on her little time line of Cass's last day. *Unsub takes her.*

Why wasn't it *Wells takes her?*

Why was she using the word *unsub?* That meant unknown subject. She was a journalist. She'd done crime stories. She wasn't going to use a word like that incorrectly.

Unless . . .

Paul's eyes flew to the third bulletin board, the one labeled with a question mark. But before he could move toward it, he was distracted by the sound of pounding footsteps and the bang of the porch screen door.

He turned around just as Abby burst into the study, her red hair a wild tangle around her redder face. She must've sprinted the entire way here. Probably to stop him from seeing . . . whatever *this* was.

The sickness churned inside him. He could feel that weight on his chest, pressing into his shoulders, like the vest was still there. *Fuck.* He needed to get out of here before he made a fool of himself.

But that required looking at her, and when his eyes finally met hers, all his resolve weakened.

And then she said the one thing that strengthened it like steel:

"I can explain."

CHAPTER 8

Abby stared at him, a horrible mix of fear, embarrassment, and defiance filling her as he looked at her.

"I don't want an explanation," he said. "I want . . ." His eyebrows drew together, and he ran his hand over his stubbled jaw. He hadn't shaved, and her eyes caught there for a moment, fixing on the strong curve of his chin. She watched as it crossed over his handsome face: that control, the calm facade, even though a storm raged in him.

"I'm getting out of here," he said firmly, walking past her, heading down the hall of the farmhouse.

And just like that, any fear or humiliation she had disappeared, and anger roared to life inside her chest like a bobcat caught in a trap. She whirled, stalking after him. He'd already made it to the porch, and she slammed through the screen door so hard it rattled on the hinges.

"Don't you *dare* walk away from me!" she spat at his back. "Not after what happened last time."

He froze. The air seemed to go from hot and muggy to ice in just seconds as he turned, his eyes burning with the anger she was feeling.

"That's low, Abby," he said, but he wasn't walking away now.

"I don't care," she said. She couldn't. She would use his guilt because she needed his help. "You owe me."

"What do you want?" he asked, incredulous. "This is ghoulish." He gestured behind her, meaning the house, her room, the board she'd set up, detailing the time lines. All the evidence. "That's no way to honor her. This isn't healthy."

"Are you kidding me?" Now she was the incredulous one. She stomped down the steps of the porch, standing on the third to last one, so they were eye to eye. God, she'd always hated how much taller he was when they were kids. He used to pick her up and swing her over his shoulders until she got sick from laughing so hard.

"I am a journalist," she hissed right in his face. "Your life may be all about justice, Paul, but mine's about *truth*."

"What the hell kind of truth are you looking for in there?" he asked, his voice rising, his eyes getting bright under the flickering porch light. "We know the truth. Cass's killer is rotting in prison where he belongs. What could there possibly be left to investigate here?"

She took a deep breath. It was now or never. He probably wouldn't believe her. It would likely be the straw that broke the camel's back. But she had to try. He was her Hail Mary.

"Howard Wells did not kill Cass," she said. "The other girls? The twelve young women before her? Those women, he killed. But he never saw Cass's face until Sheriff Baker showed him her photo in the interrogation room."

There it was. That *look*. It was concern. It was confused. And it told her that he thought she was out of her mind.

"What are you talking about? Of course he killed Cass. There was dirt from the Martins' orchard mixed with O positive blood in his truck when he was discovered."

This was her tipping point. She could crumble under his disdain, his confusion. She could let herself be swayed.

But then whoever *really* killed Cass was still walking free. And if Abby's suspicions were right, he was going to hurt another girl.

She had to rise. To stand strong.

She had to do the one thing that she *knew* he couldn't resist. Because Paul Harrison was a lot of things, but he was also still that little boy who used to tug her pigtails and chase her through the orchard rows. And he'd walk away from a lot of things. But he couldn't walk away from a challenge.

She met his eyes, her gaze steady and unflinching. "I loved Cass," she said, the truth in her words an almost painful, physical thing, hanging between them. "She was my sister in every way but blood. I've lost a lot in this world, Paul. But losing Cass will always be the hardest. I would never do anything to dishonor her or her memory or what happened. I didn't set out to find this. All I wanted to do was tell Cass's story. The problem is the story of her murder doesn't make sense when you have all the pieces spread out in front of you. And if you actually went into my study with an open mind, you would see that. So maybe you should come inside and actually *use* that big, bad FBI-trained brain of yours to do some real police work."

She could see a muscle in his jaw twitching as he ground his teeth together, fighting the urge to walk away.

So instead of waiting, she walked back up the

porch steps and went inside. She didn't need to turn around to know he was following her.

She knew him.

She was still running on anger as she entered her father's—well, now it was hers—study. She was simmering with it, but when she slid open the double wood doors, something inside her began to settle.

She was right. And if he was any kind of FBI agent, he'd see that.

The boy she'd grown up with had been smart. He had a keen mind paired with a protective instinct that sometimes got him into a little too much trouble. He'd taken on bullies and bad-asses, anyone who picked on the little guy or the vulnerable. Half of the girls in their high school had been in love with him, and when Cass chose him—because Cass was too independent to be chosen, *she* was the one who did the choosing—it had made sense, the two of them together.

"Where do you want to start?" His voice was like ice, and his expression was even colder as he stalked into the study, folding his arms across his chest. Every part of him was stiff and guarded, like he expected her to attack with her body, with her words, with whatever truth he didn't want to believe what she'd found.

"Two years ago," she said, going over to the first whiteboard and flipping it over to reveal the other side. The beginning of *her* time line, the one that had set her on this path. "Mr. Martin died. Did you know?"

He nodded. "I sent flowers."

Of course he did. Along with a handwritten note, she was sure. He probably called Cass's mom after the funeral, to check in on her. That was the way he was.

"Mrs. Martin asked to see me, after the funeral," Abby explained. "She said that out of respect for Earl, she'd promised herself she'd never ask unless he went first."

"Ask what?"

Abby gestured to the chair, an old oak rolling chair from the '30s, with studded leather and worn arms from generations of her family patriarchs, from her great-grandfather to her father, sitting in it. He sat down, still grim and unresponsive. Abby bit her lip, knowing she had her work in front of her, convincing him. But at least he was listening.

"She asked me to write Cass's story," Abby said. "She wanted me to write a book."

"And you decided to take the angle that Wells didn't kill Cass?" The incredulity was thick in his voice. It made her skin prickle with irritation. Like he thought she was some pulp writer out to get a scandalous story.

"I set out to write a book about how Cass lived, not how she died," Abby said. "But in order to do that, I had to know everything about the days leading up to that night. About Wells. About the case."

"So you went digging, and like all amateurs, you think you find something the pros overlooked," he said.

She gritted her teeth, telling herself that this had come as a shock. That he was processing. She hadn't wanted to believe it at first, either. There was comfort in knowing that Cass's killer was behind bars, that he was being punished. The idea that he was walking free . . .

It had made her sick to even contemplate it at first. The only thing that got her through it was the knowledge that if the truth still needed to be uncovered, she was the only one searching for it. This was her mission now. It was a promise she'd never made to Cass, but one that was the solemn vow to her memory that now led her life.

She would find Cass's killer. And she would make sure he paid.

"Okay, just tell me what your smoking gun is," Paul said, yanking his hand through his hair in that agitated way that told her he wanted to be anywhere but here.

"It wasn't just one thing," Abby said. "Not at first. Have you ever looked at the case? The FBI files on him? You must have access to it."

Something in his eyes flared, something that made her stomach leap like she'd just missed a step down the stairs and was falling in the worst way. "I worked hard to move on, Abby."

So he hadn't ever looked at them? God, she wouldn't have been able to resist. But she guessed that was the difference between them. She had that curiosity, that burning need to know, to uncover, no matter the cost to herself. She'd never been very good at self-preservation. It was what had led her to this mess she was in now. But if he'd never even looked at the files . . . that made what she needed to ask him to do even harder.

"Sheriff Baker is the one who did the initial processing and questioning of Wells," Abby said. "I got my hands on the video. It took me a few views to see why it was weird."

"Show me," Paul said.

He probably wanted to just look at the video so he could dismiss it and her theories, but she didn't care. If he saw the video, he was going to see what she'd seen.

She hurried over to her laptop on the desk, turning it around so it was facing him, bringing up the video file and pressing *Play*. She circled around the desk, standing behind him as it began to play.

The video was old and light was bad, but Howard Wells was sitting there, handcuffed in the Castella Rock sheriff's station. Sheriff Baker, a tall, lean man with a somber face who always reminded Abby of a melting candle, came into view. He sat down across from Wells, shuffling the paper for long moments before he finally spoke.

"Do you know why you're here?"

"Why don't you tell me?" Howard asked.

Another long silence, more paper shuffling. Even after watching the video what felt like hundreds of times, Abby *still* felt annoyed at the obvious way the sheriff was trying to intimidate him. It was pitiful, and she could see it on Wells's face. What he thought of Baker. What he thought of this whole thing.

He wasn't panicked. He wasn't scared.

No, he was *amused*.

Abby watched as the sheriff began to question Wells. As he pushed the photo of Cass across the table, his voice rising as he demanded that Wells admit that he'd killed her.

"Why would I kill such a sweet thing?" Wells asked.

"She has the mark on her," Baker said on the video. "The *X*. *Your* mark. And we found dirt from the orchard she lives on in your truck, along with blood. So how do you explain that?"

"There," Abby said, pointing to the screen.

Wells's face shifted. It was just a flash, so subtle that she'd almost missed it the first time.

"He made a face," Paul said. "Lots of people make faces when they realize they're caught."

"Wait," Abby said, pressing Play again. They watched as Baker basically lobbed question after question about Cass to Wells for a good ten minutes. And then a man in a black suit came into the interrogation room, clearly an FBI agent, and the video suddenly cut off.

"I'm not terribly compelled, Abby," Paul said.

Abby gritted her teeth. "I'm not finished, Paul," she shot back, wishing they were eight again and she could solve things by pushing him into a mud puddle. "So you've seen the Baker interrogation. Now it's time to look at the FBI interrogation."

He sat up straighter in the chair. "How the hell did you get the FBI tapes?" he demanded.

"I have my ways," Abby said.

"You do realize your ways are illegal?" he asked.

Such a Boy Scout. Even now. It would annoy her if it wasn't so damn *him*. Instead, it made her feel warm inside, like something familiar and good was wrapped around her. Which was rich, considering he was glaring at her for illegally procuring FBI tapes.

"Just watch the tape. And tell me what you think."

Instead of watching the video this time, she watched Paul. His face. She watched, listening as the FBI began a much more nuanced interrogation, and she wondered if he'd see what she'd seen.

Wells was no longer silently amused, as he was with Baker. But the FBI didn't put him on edge.

No, the FBI was Wells's stage. And he was performing.

He was telling them *everything*.

Paul's eyebrows snapped together when Wells mentioned Cass's soccer uniform. Cass had to quit soccer at the beginning of the year because she'd strained her Achilles tendon. But the picture that Sheriff Baker had shoved toward Wells had been one of Cass in her soccer uniform.

Then Paul's eyes narrowed as Wells talked about leaving Cass's body back in the orchard, his breath changing when Wells talked about laying her beneath the almond trees.

Cass's family grew olives, not almonds. But Sheriff Baker had mistakenly said *almond orchard* in his interrogation with Wells.

Baker had given Wells all the information he needed to claim Cass as his victim.

When it was done, Abby reached over and closed the laptop.

Paul was quiet, his fingers tight around the arms of the chair. Abby let him stew in his silence for a moment, because she knew what he was feeling. He was fighting against it, because the idea that Cass's killer had been walking around free all these years?

That was a bitter pill to swallow.

"Okay," he said finally. "It is weird. But his confession—"

"Is not real," Abby said. "You saw exactly what I did, didn't you? He manipulated Sheriff Baker into giving him all the information he needed to claim Cass's murder as his—and then he turned around and used that information to convince the FBI he was the killer."

"It could just be a coincidence. Or one of his games," Paul said.

Abby took a deep breath. "It's not. I know. Because I went to see him."

"What?" He was up and out of his chair so fast, so smoothly, that she nearly startled like a deer. He wasn't looming over her in an intimidating way, no, instead, he reached out, fingers closing gently over her hand, like he needed to suddenly reassure himself that she was whole, that she was here.

That Wells hadn't taken her too.

Heat spread through her at the simple touch. There were calluses on his hands, but not in the places she remembered. They rode rough on his trigger finger now, instead of on his palm. His tool was a gun now, not a shovel.

"What the hell were you thinking?" he demanded.

"I was thinking I needed confirmation," Abby said, her chin jutting out stubbornly. "I needed to be sure. And now I am."

"How did you even get access to him? I have explicit orders that anyone visiting him has to—"

Her eyes widened. "Oh, so I'm the ghoulish one for researching this, but *you* somehow control who he does and doesn't see? How did you manage that?"

His cheeks turned ruddy, his blue eyes sweeping down. "I'm one of the FBI's top supervisory agents, Abby. I have a lot of friends."

"I can't believe you," she said. "How can you . . ." She made herself stop and take a deep breath. She had to stay in control. "My conversation with him was illuminating. It confirmed that he had never seen Cass before that day Sheriff Baker pushed her photo across the interrogation table."

"How can you be sure?" Paul asked.

"Her hair," Abby said.

His frown deepened. "Her hair," he echoed.

"During our meeting, he was looking to get a rise out of me, and I wasn't giving it to him," Abby explained. "So he started going on about what drew him to Cass. He kept talking about her curls."

"Her curls . . . but she straightened her hair."

"Exactly," Abby said. "Look." She went over to her board, flipping it again, revealing the photo of Cass in her soccer uniform, her many-ringleted ponytail hanging behind her as she smiled at the camera. "She has curls in this photo. The photo Baker showed him. If he saw her in real life—if he *stalked* her like he did with his other victims?—he would've known she wore her hair straight. He would've known she didn't play soccer that whole year. He would've known he put her body in an olive orchard, not an almond orchard. There's a giant sign on the Martin Orchard gate that says MARTIN FAMILY OLIVE ORCHARD, for goodness' sake! He played them. All of them. He played us. He did not kill her."

She looked at him, at his handsome face that seemed to be warring with his mind right now. She needed him to believe her. She needed his help.

She needed someone who had loved Cass as much as she had. She needed him to fight for Cass as hard as she was.

"Then why did he confess?" Paul demanded. "It's all well and good to say that the confession is a bit weird. I acknowledge that. But *why* would he confess?"

"Because he's protecting someone," Abby said. "Cass's real killer."

CHAPTER 9

This one looks so sweet.

They always do, at the end. So peaceful, as he shovels the dirt carefully over them.

This is a reverent time. Where they join with the earth again, finally returned, because of him.

They're rarely grateful, even though they should be. This one wasn't. The fierce little thing fought him.

But he always wins. Just ask Dr. X.

He's French-braided this one's hair, weaved it in double plaits pulled over the shoulders the way *she* used to wear it. He reaches out, stroking his finger down the length of the braid, the ends curling around his finger.

It's so bittersweet, saying goodbye.

But the fruit is ripened on the vine. The leaves will yellow soon, the days growing shorter and colder. Soon, snow will fall, and the ground will be too hard to dig for months.

It's a time for new things. New growth. A new plaything.

He already knows exactly which one he's going to pick. He's been watching. He's been waiting.

He pats the dirt down with the shovel, smoothing it over as he begins to hum. Tossing the shovel to the side, he makes his way over to the pile of stones, taking them one by one and laying them carefully over the lonely grave, in the middle of the forest, where no one will ever find it.

"Oh, Danny boy." His voice floats up, rising among the tall trees . . .

He continues to sing, assembling the stones in a large X over her body.

The harvest is coming soon.

He needs to be ready.

CHAPTER 10

Paul felt like he'd been hit by a truck. Like he'd just done an Ironman. He'd done the triathlon in his twenties, and the way his body felt right now was similar: exhausted, shaky, and sliding into a numb state of overwhelmed shock.

He had thought Abby was just living in the past. He'd been so angry.

And now . . .

Now he was staring at evidence. It wasn't hard, but it was real. He couldn't deny that now. Any agent worth his salt would find Wells's confession suspect when compared side by side with Sheriff Baker's interrogation. He was betting the agents in charge of the original investigation had only glanced at Baker's transcripts—they may have never even seen the tape or realized that Baker had unwittingly fed Wells information he hadn't acquired yet.

Christ. This was a disaster. The idea of Abby breathing the same air as Wells—of him even *looking* at her—filled him with a raging anger that almost obliterated everything else he was feeling.

Another killer. A partner? Is that what she was talking about? His mind began to work through the possibilities, shifting through and rejecting options and ideas. If Wells had a partner he was trying to protect, that meant Wells was the leader in the relationship. That meant his partner was the follower.

But if Wells's partner had set him up for Cass's murder, that was far from following Wells's lead.

Were they dealing with two dominant personalities? Or a follower/leader partnership that morphed into leader/leader? Had the student become the master and decided there could only be one?

"Why would he protect someone who framed him?" Paul asked Abby.

"I don't know," Abby said. "But I think I know how they met."

Of course she did. Paul briefly wondered if it was just his lot in life to be surrounded by tenacious, brilliant women. He seemed to be built for it, he thought as he got to his feet and walked over to the evidence board.

"I talked to everyone who'd ever had a connection with Wells," Abby said. The doorbell rang, and Abby jerked in her seat, whirling around.

"Abby?" That was his sister Georgia's voice. "Paul? You two aren't doing something dirty, are you?"

"Just a second, Georgia!" Abby called, scrambling to her feet. "Come on," she said. "Do you want her to see? We have to get back."

Paul hesitated, torn, but Abby glared at him and he followed, closing the double doors of the study behind him.

His sister was standing in Abby's foyer, her arms crossed over her chest, an amused look on her face. "What was taking you two so long?"

"Oh, we just got to talking about old times," Abby said smoothly. "The rest of the soda's in the shed, I'll go grab it."

She hurried out the back door, and Georgia pursed her lips in a knowing smile.

"Don't look at me like that," Paul said.

"Like what?" his sister asked innocently. She was three years his senior and was serving her third term as mayor of Castella Rock, which didn't stop her from trying to meddle in *everyone's* business.

"Like you just caught me with my pants down," he said.

Her smile grew wider. She took after their mom, with her brown hair and blue eyes and sweet face. Paul was all their father—tall and broad and very blond. "I did no such thing," she said. "I just think it would be nice if you found someone to settle down with."

Paul's stomach tightened, and suddenly all he could think of was that night. The last time he saw Abby. That last fight. How it ended.

"Drop it, Georgia," he said, maybe a little too sharply, as Abby came back into the house, her arms full of the crates. He hurried over to help her, thankful that Georgia didn't say anything else, just helped them bring the soda back to the meadow.

As he went through the motions of the party, smiling and laughing, greeting and hugging people he hadn't seen for a few years, his mind was racing—his body felt surreal, like he wasn't really inside it.

When he finally had a moment to escape, he crossed the meadow to the tree line, far enough out of earshot of everyone as the music rose and the sun set. He pulled his phone out of his pocket and dialed a number.

"Hey, it's me," he said, when she picked up. "I need you to do something for me. And I need you to do it quietly."

"Sure, boss."

"Get me every file we have on Howard Wells aka Dr. X," Paul said. "Then get on a plane. You're coming to California."

CHAPTER 11

Abby woke up the next morning to a knock on her door, followed by Roscoe barking, the sound of his paws skittering down the stairs. Feeling like she hadn't slept a wink, she squinted at her alarm, realizing she'd forgotten to set it. It was nearly nine.

The knocking increased, along with Roscoe's barking.

Abby threw on one of the embroidered robes she'd gotten at one of those rummage sales on Orchard Row that were filled with treasures long forgotten in attics. Tying the length of dark blue silk around her waist, she hurried downstairs, trying to finger-comb her bedhead into some sort of order as she did.

"Roscoe, in the kitchen!" she ordered the dog. He looked disappointed that he couldn't keep barking, but obeyed, trotting down the hall.

She opened the door, raising an eyebrow

when she saw a petite girl with a cotton-candy pink bob and big, wide eyes standing there. She was wearing a circle skirt from the '50s that had little bows painted all over it and a dotted Swiss blouse tucked into it. She managed to look modern and vintage at the same time, a curious combination that was charming with her doll-like prettiness and sharp smile.

"Hi," Abby said.

"Hi!" chirped the girl. She couldn't be more than twenty-three. "So, where can I set up?"

Abby frowned. "Set up?"

"I'm Zooey," she said. When Abby continued to stare at her, she said, "Has Paul called you?"

"My phone's upstairs. I'm sorry . . . who are you?" Abby asked.

"Special Technical Consultant and Head Forensic Expert Zooey Phillips," she said, holding out her hand.

Abby took it, shaking it. "Nice to meet you," she said.

"So, where's the evidence board I've heard about?" Zooey asked as Abby held the door open wider, letting her in.

"Everything's set up in the study," Abby said. She looked down at her robe and ran her hand through her hair again. She must look a mess, but she didn't really want to leave this girl alone with her evidence. She looked so *young*. How could she be head of forensics already? "Is Paul coming?"

"I think so," Zooey said. "Study this way?" She pointed.

Abby nodded, following her down the hallway, opening the double doors. She'd opened the windows last night to let the cool air in, and the curtains were still drawn, letting light spill in the room. It made it look less gloomy, until you noticed what exactly was on those whiteboards.

She felt more than a little nervous as Zooey strode into the study and looked at the boards. Abby knew she was no FBI agent, but she'd worked hard on covering as much ground as possible. She'd done all right, she liked to think.

But the look on Paul's face when he originally saw the boards . . . she wasn't sure she'd ever be able to erase that from her mind. The hurt, the horror, the realization.

He still believed her, though. He had to, if he'd sent Zooey here.

The girl let out a low whistle. "Wow, he wasn't lying. You've been busy."

Abby shrugged. "I'm a journalist," she said, by way of explanation.

"I know," Zooey said. "I read your piece on

the rising maternal death rate in America on the drive here. It was so great I went back and read most of your work. I'm a bit of a fangirl now."

Abby smiled. "Well, that's nice. Thanks," she said, wondering if Zooey was just flattering her in order to put her at ease. And then she mentally winced at herself. She needed to stop being so suspicious.

"I've brought some stuff from DC," Zooey said, patting the satchel she had slung over her shoulder. "But the boss will be pissed if I show you before he's here. Protocol and all."

"Paul is a stickler for rules," Abby said.

"Some of the time," Zooey replied with a smile. "Me being here? Definitely against protocol."

Abby gestured for her to sit, and took the seat across from her. "He's not going to get in trouble, is he?" she asked, concerned. She didn't want Paul doing something stupid like risking his job for this.

Zooey shook her head, pursing her scarlet lips. "Nah. He's basically the agency's golden boy. I mean, he looks like Captain America *and* he acts like him. What more could anyone want?"

Abby couldn't help but smile at the description. "I like that. Captain America. His nickname around here used to be *Boy Scout.*" She didn't mention she was the one who gave it to him all those years ago.

Zooey smiled, clearly delighted with this piece of information.

"So, Head Forensic Expert," Abby said. "That's impressive."

"For someone so young?" Zooey asked, her eyes dancing.

Something told Abby she got this kind of comment a lot. "Sorry," she said. "I just . . . how old are you?"

"Twenty-two," the girl replied.

Abby frowned. "I thought the FBI had age requirements."

"They do," Zooey nodded. "Not so much for me, though."

So Paul had called in a girl genius who looked like she'd stepped out of a punky Doris Day world?

"I'm very good at my job," Zooey assured her.

"I'm sure you are," Abby said. "I really don't mean to question your skill. I'm . . . this whole thing . . . it's been a long week," she finally managed to say.

Zooey shot her a sympathetic look, reaching out and patting her hand. "I understand," she said. "You did something pretty incredible, Abby. You saw something no one else did. All the experts, all the lawyers, and none of them saw what you did."

THERE WAS KNOCKING at the front door, followed by Roscoe barking and dashing out of the kitchen to confront the new person in his territory.

"Hey, buddy, it's just me," Abby heard Paul's voice say. Then footsteps, and he was in the doorway of the study, wearing a plaid flannel shirt and jeans that had holes in the knee and he looked so much like himself, so much like the boy she remembered, her heart stuttered in her chest for a moment.

"Whoa, boss, you've gone all country," Zooey said. "Are those *cowboy boots*?" She whipped her phone out, taking a picture, cackling, when Paul shot her a disapproving look.

"Did you bring everything?" he asked.

Zooey nodded. "Can I set up in here?"

"Let's do it," he said.

The girl pulled a laptop and a digital projector out of her bag, setting them on Abby's father's old cherrywood desk and sitting down at it. "This is gonna take a few minutes," she said.

"Do you want something to drink or eat?" Abby asked, finally remembering her manners.

She realized once again she was still in her pajamas.

"I'm fine," Zooey replied.

"I'm going to get dressed," Abby said.

She had almost escaped down the hall when Paul's voice stopped her at the foot of the stairs. She sighed, closing her eyes and steeling herself before she turned around.

"I'm sorry," he said.

Of all the things she was expecting, that was the last thing she could've imagined.

"I shouldn't have been so derisive about your theory at first," he said. "You were right."

"Thank you," she said.

"This is going to be difficult," he said. "I spent last night going through the FBI file on Cass. There are crime scene photos. I wanted to warn you before Zooey let you look at it."

There he went again, trying to protect her like she was still a little girl. A part of her prickled at the idea that she needed a warning. Another part felt the warm glow of safety. And yet another part was grateful, because there are some things you cannot unsee. And your best friend's body is one of them.

"I'll be right down," she said as her answer, and he didn't try to stop her again as she went up the stairs.

By the time Abby got back downstairs, Zooey had everything ready, her projector set up to beam against the wall behind the desk.

"I took down the painting," Zooey said, gesturing to the oil painting Abby's great-grandfather had done of his hunting dogs back in the day. "I hope that's okay."

"It's fine," Abby said, taking the painting and setting it out of the way. "So, how does this start?"

"I had Zooey pull up all the FBI files on Dr. X. Not just Cass's case, but the other twelve girls."

"I read them on the plane," Zooey said.

"All of them?" Abby asked, shocked.

"I read fast," Zooey replied. "So here's the thing." She tapped on the portable keyboard in her hand, and photos of thirteen girls suddenly appeared on the wall. All of them had long, dark hair, and Cass's photo was at the bottom of the row, with a red circle around it. "Cass was definitely X's type. He likes sweet-faced brunettes. But there are a few things that stand out about Cass."

"Like what?"

"All the others have girls who have dark eyes," Zooey explained.

"When there's no variety like that, in such a

large victim pool, that tells us that he has a very specific type. Deviating from that even a little is unusual," Paul added.

"That makes sense," Abby said. "But we already know that X didn't kill Cass."

"This is about the other guy," Zooey said. "See, if we can narrow down the differences between Cass and X's victims, then we can start to form a victim profile for our unsub."

"Normally, our profiler does this," Paul told Abby. "But she's on another case."

"And I've been working with Grace, learning profiling and experimenting with some algorithms," Zooey said. "I've got five variables where Cass doesn't match X's other victims." She punched a few keys, and the girls' photos disappeared, and a list appeared.

Eye Color
Athleticism
Only Child
Two Parent Household
Family Economic Status

"So, you're saying *these* things are why the unsub took Cass?" Abby asked. How could she be sure? It seemed like such an arbitrary list.

"Maybe," Paul said. "He may not recognize that he has preferences. Or he may be aware of them. It depends on how sophisticated he is."

"Oh, he's sophisticated," Zooey said.

Paul frowned at her. "What do you mean?" he asked.

"I didn't want to tell you until my program finished running," Zooey explained. "But I put Code Sibyl on it."

"Zooey," Paul broke in, and there was warning in his voice. "That's not approved yet."

"Only because the government is slow," Zooey said. "Do you want to know what I found?"

"What's Code Sibyl?" Abby hated this feeling of being in the dark.

"It's a computer program I designed," Zooey said. "To catch serial killers."

"You're kidding me." Abby looked at Paul, like, *who the hell is this person?*

He sighed. "It analyzes a killer's victimology and preferences, and identifies potential victims by working through all the records on John and Jane Does, current cases, cold cases, missing persons reports, etc. It hasn't been field-tested yet."

"Well, I kind of did a field test. On the plane," Zooey broke in.

"What did you find?" Paul asked.

"Our guy's been busy," Zooey said, and on the far wall, seven girls' pictures appeared. "Meet the missing girls of I-5. The stretch of highway that goes through here, all the way up to Oregon, is full of transients, runaways, hitchhikers, campers, bicyclists, you name it. It has over a dozen rest stops, at least a hundred gas stations, thousands of acres of national forest and parks, and tons of outdoor attractions. And there are stretches where it's nothing but deep forest for miles. It's an active stretch of highway, so there's a normal amount of criminal activity and accidents. But then, I went back fifteen years. I plugged in Dr. X's victimology *combined* with Cass's differences from the girls."

She pulled up a map of Northern California on the projector. There were seven red dots along the stretch of highway she'd highlighted. "Every two years, since Cass's murder, a girl has gone missing on the I–5. Jessica Adams went missing on a camping trip in the Trinities with her parents. The rangers thought she'd gotten lost and must've died out there in the woods. Talia Hernandez was on a school trip to Mt. Shasta when she got separated from her group.

No one ever saw her again. Ramona Quinn was a runaway from Chico who was last seen at the Castella rest stop by a trucker she'd hitched a ride with. Molly Bailes was working at the ski resort and never showed up for her shift. She commuted to work, on the 5, but no one ever found her car. Kathy Dove was an aspiring photographer who went out to take pictures of some of the old bridges and never came back. Imogen Meade was an experienced equestrian who did trail rides. They found her horse—they never found her. And finally, Keira Rice, she went missing almost two years ago, at a soccer meet in Yreka. She hurt her ankle during the match and her roommate said she went to get ice for it from the machine at their motel. They found the ice bucket at the bottom of the stairs."

Abby stared at the girl's faces, chills running through her entire body.

They all looked *so much* like Cass. She'd even remembered hearing about Keira Rice—she'd lived in the next county over—when she first went missing, and she'd remembered praying that her family would find her.

There was a slamming sound, and Abby startled when she realized Paul had left the room abruptly, the double doors of the study rattling as he closed them behind him.

Zooey's eyes—already so big and doll-like—widened even more. "Shit," she said. "I . . . maybe I should have approached that better."

It took her a second to recover, because she was feeling struck dumb. Seven girls? Were there even more, if they went back further? How long had Cass's killer been in this area, slowly picking off the young women who suited his sick needs, doing it in such a clever, random way that no one suspected the connection until this girl with pink hair plugged a bunch of lines of code into a database.

Abby's head was spinning, but she needed to get it together. She needed to get Paul back inside—and back in the game.

"I'll go talk to him," Abby said. "Just stay here. There's drinks and apple pie and a ton of leftover BBQ in the fridge if you're hungry."

"I didn't mean to—" Zooey started, and her mouth drooped, and Abby once again realized how very young she was. She might be brilliant, but she was a baby in some ways, still. And she clearly idolized Paul as a boss.

"Don't worry," Abby assured her with a tight smile. "He's just . . . he cares. A lot."

"I know," Zooey said. "He recruited me. I was on a . . . not so good path. He kind of saved me."

"He has a history of doing that," Abby said.

"Maybe someday we'll share some stories. I'll be right back."

She left Zooey behind in the study, and made her way out of the farmhouse, down the porch steps, and across the field, toward the orchard, knowing he'd seek refuge there.

CHAPTER 12

Seven girls. And that was likely just the beginning. If Zooey had only gone back fifteen years with her program . . .

Paul clenched his fists, breathing hard as he paced up and down the orchard row, trying to calm himself.

How had he let this happen? That's all he could think right now. He'd never looked at FBI files on Cass or Dr. X. He'd avoided them, even when his mentor, Frank Edenhurst, had offered to give him access. He'd been selfish. If he hadn't . . .

Would he have seen what Abby had? Would he have been whole enough? Or would he have denied the truth because it was easier? Because the idea of Cass's killer walking free . . .

Fifteen years. Fifteen years and at least seven other girls, and it was *his fault*.

God, the weight was pushing down on his

chest again. He pressed his hand over his heart, trying to slow his breathing.

This was his fault. Those girls . . . his mind began to sift through the facts that Zooey had thrown at him, filing impressions and theories in different categories as he sorted through it, picturing the map Zooey had shown them in his mind.

He'd taken girls from five different counties. And some of them were assumed lost instead of kidnapped.

No one would've seen the pattern. Especially because their bodies never showed up.

His stomach clenched. He was a realist. He knew the statistics. For every Jaycee Duggard who survived, there were hundreds of girls dead hours, days, weeks, months after they were taken.

There were seven dead girls somewhere. Probably lost in the acres of national forest surrounding them, never to be found. The tangle of mountains that bordered the valley were wild and vast, some places impossible to reach any way but on foot.

"Paul." Abby's voice broke through the churning guilt filling him. He turned. She was at the end of the row, her eyes brimming with an emotion he couldn't quite identify.

Without another word, she walked toward him, taking his head in her hands, resting her forehead against his.

Everything inside him untwined and settled, his eyes closing as her fingers threaded through his hair.

He didn't know how long they stood there, pressed together. It could've been minutes. It felt like hours.

She smelled like honey and lemons, like he remembered, and he couldn't stop himself from reaching up and cupping her cheek.

The callus on his thumb caught against the softness of her cheekbone, and there it was, stirring to life inside him, the thing that he'd buried, tamped down, and tried so damn hard to ignore throughout the years.

Need. Want. Desire.

She'd tugged at his heart, at his gut, at everything in him, his very soul, for so damn long. And he'd denied it for just as long. He'd run from it as a teenager and as an adult. Every time. He'd loved other women. And he'd never be unfaithful in his mind or his heart.

But Abby . . .

Abby was his childhood. She was the trip across the meadow—867 steps when he was a boy, lessening with each year as he grew taller and taller. She was muddy red hair tangled in his face, freckled hands holding his as his father left to get sober. She was his first kiss at six and sometimes, in the deep night, when he'd jerked awake with the phantom weight of the suicide vest pressing on him, the only thing that soothed him was the thought about her being his last.

It was so damn hard to deny it when she was right here. When he was so close. When he could just lean forward and . . .

"It's going to be okay," Abby murmured, and Paul felt a flash of disgust at himself for feeling this way.

She'd made it very clear, a long time ago, that they were just friends. And that anything otherwise would be dishonoring Cass's memory.

"Yeah," he said, reluctantly pulling away from her. "It will be. I'm going to take over from here."

Her eyebrows knit together. "Take over . . ." she echoed.

"You're a civilian, Abby," he said. "You could get hurt."

Her mouth dropped open in an outraged *O*. "You don't get to say when I stop being involved here."

Of course Abby had no qualms about hunting down a serial killer. She probably pulled the rifle her daddy got her when she was sixteen out of the gun safe just for the occasion. She had always been fearless. The girl who jumped off the highest rocks at the swimming hole and told the best ghost stories around the bonfire and who had beaten him to the punch—literally—when Danny Roberts had slept with his sister Faye and then slut-shamed her all over school. Danny's nose was permanently hooked to the right now, courtesy of Abby.

"I'm the FBI," he said. "I kind of do."

"Bullshit," she declared. "I know you, Harrison. You work with that famous profiler. The one who specializes in serial killers. Grace Sinclair. I read her novels. If this was something you wanted your entire team on, you would've called her in. Instead, you called in your girl genius because she hero-worships you. She's not gonna blab to your higher-ups about what you're up to on your vacation. This is off the books—until you've got concrete evidence to take to them."

Paul bit the inside of his cheek, wishing she wasn't so damn alluring when she was reading him like a book. "You're a brat," he said.

Her mouth twisted into a wry smile. "I do what I have to."

"You know, it's against the law to blackmail an FBI agent," he said.

"I'm not blackmailing you," she scoffed. "It's not my fault if I'm more clever than you. Now are you gonna come back inside?"

He looked past her shoulder to the farmhouse in the distance, feeling the dread start to build.

Usually, the spur of the hunt, the methodical steps that it took to find a killer, was something that motivated and fueled him. But he had a horrible feeling, one that had been there from the moment he realized that Abby was right . . .

There was more to this story. More to Cass's murder than they ever thought.

That meant secrets were going to be uncovered. And secrets in a small town ran deep.

"Let's go," he said.

CHAPTER 13

"Oh, good, you're back."

Zooey had helped herself to a piece of apple pie from the fridge and perched on the edge of the desk to eat it. "This is delicious," she told Abby, pointing her fork at the plate.

"Thanks," Abby said.

"You mad at me, boss?" Zooey asked.

Paul shook his head. "I'm not mad at you, Zo. It's just a shock. Everything I thought I knew is wrong."

"I'm sorry," Zooey said. "Both of you. I know that Cass was special to you. And from what I've read, she was a special person all around. It sucks that we're here. But now that we are, we can figure out what really happened—and maybe prevent another girl from being taken."

Abby felt a chill down her spine. "Another girl?" she echoed.

"Well, yeah," Zooey said. "If the seven girls I identified are his victims, then he's operating on a really predictable two-year schedule. He takes a girl every other fall. We're a bit overdue, actually. Ramona, Molly, and Imogen were all taken in early September. But Keira, if she is his seventh victim, was taken in late November."

"It's November fifth," Abby said, horrified at the thought that some girl was walking around right now, unknowing a psychopath was closing in on her.

"We've got a ticking clock then," Paul said grimly.

"That's my thinking," Zooey said.

Abby had to clench her hands because they were starting to shake. Maybe she didn't have the stomach for this, but it didn't matter anymore: She was in it, and she was going to see it through. For Cass.

"Zooey, how accurate is your Sibyl program?" Abby asked. "Can we be sure *all* these girls are the unsub's victims?"

Zooey shook her head. "This is the Code Sibyl's first outing. Programs like this are always going to have bugs I have to work out. I'm human and I make mistakes. And the records that Sibyl's scanning through aren't perfect either. But it gives us a rough place to start to do some good old-fashioned police work. Sibyl's designed to be an aid, not a complete solution."

"Speaking of that," Paul said. "Have you tracked down the girls' families yet?"

"I've sent the address of Keira Rice's parents to your phone," Zooey said. "They're about an hour's drive from here."

Paul turned to Abby, and there was a glitter of challenge in his eyes that made sparks go off under her skin. "You up for a little gumshoeing?" he asked, like he hadn't just demanded she leave the case behind fifteen minutes ago. What was *with* him?

"I am," she said.

"I'm gonna step out and make a call," Paul said. "My mom's gonna be pissed that I'm ditching lunch with her."

"Tell Tandy hi," Abby called after him.

He disappeared out of the study, and Zooey pursed her lips, making a tutting sound like a little old lady. "Wow, you two have *tension*," she commented.

Abby could feel her cheeks getting hot. She couldn't believe she was getting called out by a pint-sized genius with a mythology geek streak. "We've been friends a long time," she said, simply.

"That is *not* the way a guy looks at you when he's feeling just friendly," Zooey said, with an air of precocious wisdom that was so cute Abby couldn't help but smile. She liked this kid. She had gumption.

"He's just being a hard-ass," Abby said. "He likes being in charge."

"Well, after the whole bomb thing, can you really blame him?" Zooey asked, hopping off the desk. She was halfway across the room when she froze, catching sight of the look on Abby's face.

"What *'bomb thing'*?" Abby demanded, feeling like someone had thrown ice water in her face.

"Um . . ." Zooey looked over her shoulder, like she was weighing her chances of escape. "There may have been an incident on a kidnapping case. Our kidnapping victim was diabetic, which meant we only had a small window of time to work with. The boss led a team in to get her, but everything went wrong. The kidnapper strapped him into a suicide vest full of C4 and held him hostage with the girl for like, a day. He's better, though. The PTSD was bad for a while, but he's drinking a lot less coffee now, which means he's sleeping more and wow, you look really horrified, I'm making this a whole lot worse, aren't I?" Zooey's entire monologue came out as kind of a rush and she had to take a deep breath after she was done.

"I need to sit down," Abby said. And then she did just that.

"Oh, my God, he's gonna be so mad," Zooey muttered to herself. "Look, I'm sorry. The way he looks at you and talked about you, I just figured you two were close and you probably knew the whole deal. My big mouth gets me in trouble *all* the time. Please, don't say anything to him about it. The only reason I know about the PTSD is because he doesn't believe in keeping things from his team. He held a whole meeting about it and everything."

"Someone strapped C4 to him?" Abby asked dumbly, the details Zooey had given her whirling around in her head like bats around a cave at dusk.

"It kinda goes with the job. Our team, it's an elite task force," she explained. "He is the best of the best, Abby. And sometimes, that means putting yourself into some major danger for the greater good. And the boss? He's *all* about the greater good."

"My God," Abby said. She knew, intellectually, that of course Paul's job was dangerous.

But maybe she'd tricked herself into thinking he spent most of his time behind a desk, giving orders, instead of out in the field, where even the right move could get him killed. The reality now was impossible to deny, and her heart picked up when she realized that he hadn't left the study earlier because he was angry over Code Sibyl's reveal of the possible victims.

Had he actually left because his PTSD had been triggered? He had been breathing in that long, slow way when she'd found him in the orchard. Was he trying to gain some kind of control?

She had very little experience with PTSD and her mind was racing. Had she made it worse by touching him? He would've moved away if she had, right? Abby's stomach tightened, feeling like the ground was moving beneath her, unsteady and unpredictable.

"You're not going to tell him I blabbed, are you?" Zooey asked. She looked so worried Abby shot her a reassuring smile.

"Of course not," she said. "It does explain some things, but you don't have to worry. If he wants to tell me, as far as he's concerned, that'll be the first time I'm hearing it."

"Thank you," Zooey said, letting out a sigh of

relief. She set the pie plate down on the edge of the desk. "Hey, do you mind if I ask you something about your evidence boards?"

"Sure."

"You've got a list here, on the X board." Zooey went over to the second whiteboard, tapping on a sticky note affixed to the far right corner. There was a short list scribbled on it: personals, forums, newspaper ads, dating sites. "What's this about?"

"I was trying to figure out how Wells and the unsub met," Abby explained. "How they communicated and traded information. One of my initial theories was that the reason Wells didn't give up the unsub was because he didn't know who he was."

Zooey frowned. "You think they connected online anonymously?"

Abby shrugged. "It was just a theory. One of the assistant coroners who worked with Wells in Oregon mentioned he was always buying stuff off Craigslist, so I was thinking that might be an angle, but I couldn't ever track anything solid down."

"Hmm, interesting," Zooey said. "You have your notes from that assistant coroner who mentioned Craigslist?"

"On the desktop." Abby nodded at the computer set in the corner. "It's in the Medford folder. Alfred Cooke."

"Cool, I'll look through it, see if anything jumps out at me," Zooey said.

Paul stuck his head back in the study. "I'm ready, if you are," he said.

Abby felt a flash of apprehension at the idea of just appearing on Keira Rice's family's porch, asking questions. She wasn't the kind of journalist who liked to ambush her interview subjects. She never found it led to anything productive.

"If the dog scratches at the door, just let him out," Abby said to Zooey. "He likes to wander around the orchard in the afternoon, if we don't get back."

"Call me if you find anything else," Paul told Zooey. "And if Grace calls . . ."

"I'm helping you with a family matter," Zooey said. "She's not gonna call. She and Gavin are on a case Jake O'Conner brought them. Some drug trafficking thing."

"It's about time that guy did me a favor," Paul muttered, and it made Zooey laugh and Abby frown, not getting the joke.

"Let's take your truck," Paul said.

"You think a little mud on an old Chevy's

going to make them more inclined to talk to us than pulling up in the BMW?" Abby asked, pulling her keys out and going over to her truck.

"Couldn't hurt," Paul said, climbing inside the truck. "Wow, this thing hasn't changed since the last time I was in it."

Abby's old S-10 had been the one she'd learned to drive at twelve—farm girls learned early—and the one her father had given her at sixteen. When she'd moved back home, she'd pulled it out of the back barn and started driving it again.

"Rizzo's a good ol' girl," Abby said, patting the dashboard of her Chevy.

"I'd forgotten how obsessed you were with that movie," he said, his dimples flashing as she started the car.

"Shut up," she muttered, trying not to smile herself.

"I wonder . . ." Paul said, and he reached down, tugging at something, and with a laugh, he pulled an ancient pack of American Spirits out from underneath the seat, where they'd been taped. He shook the pack at her. "Been a long time since you cleaned in here, huh, Winny?"

"Oh, my God, how *old* are those?" she asked.

"If I remember correctly, I stashed them there to avoid my mom finding them in my room when we were like, fifteen? Right after you got your learner's permit."

"If my dad had found those, he would've grounded me for weeks!" Abby said, half laughing, half outraged on her teenage self's behalf.

"And if my mom had found them in my room, I would've been grounded for *years*," Paul shot back.

"Wow, so ready to throw me under the bus," Abby drawled sarcastically, shaking her head with great exaggeration as she pulled the truck out of the driveway and made her way down the long dirt road that led to the road and highway. She felt warm inside, peaceful and just a spark of happy as they fell into an easy rhythm, like no time had passed. Like nothing had changed.

Like they'd never lost Cass or themselves or each other.

"If your father had found them, I would've been the gentleman I am," Paul said. "Fallen on my sword. Taken the blame. Been the bigger man."

She rolled her eyes. "Keep telling yourself that, buddy." She turned onto the highway, heading north, toward the mountains and Trinity County, where the Rices lived.

They fell into a silence for a while as the landscape changed from neat rows of trees for as far as the eye could see and cute little farm stands sprinkled every few miles on the road, to craggy mountains and wild tangles of pine trees scattered across them.

"Do you think she's right?" Abby asked finally, unable to stop herself. "Zooey, I mean," she added, when Paul shot her a questioning look. "About another girl going missing soon."

"We'll see," Paul said, in that way that told her the answer was *yes* and he didn't want to say it. Maybe he didn't want to break it to her—or to himself.

They fell back into silence, and this time, Abby let it go and focused on the road, on the mountains ahead, and what lay beyond.

CHAPTER 14

The Rice farm was set in the valley, near a tiny town called McCloud that was more of a gas station and a restaurant than a real town. Cattle were grazing in the rolling fields that made up the property, and the big red barn and horse paddock looked like they hadn't seen use in a while.

Abby pulled up to the front of the yellow farmhouse, where marigolds were planted in each of the window boxes, shining like little suns.

"So, let me take the lead here," Paul said. "I know you're used to interviewing people, but I'm gonna have to show them my badge. They're going to have questions."

"I understand," Abby said quickly.

"You do?" he asked, feeling surprised. He'd expected her to fight him on this. She was opinionated, Abby was. She liked to lead.

"Paul, you're an FBI agent. You're showing up

on these parents' doorstep and you don't have any news about their missing daughter, but you have a whole lot of questions about her. I don't want to step in it or accidentally give these people false hope. You have the experience to navigate this a lot better than me. I respect that."

"Thank you," he said.

"But you need to respect my instincts too," she said. "You'll be asking the questions. But me? I'm gonna be looking around as much as I can. There's a lot you can learn just by looking at a person's space."

"Fair enough," he said. "You've always had a good eye."

"Okay, then, we're agreed," she said.

"For once," he said, and then mentally winced. Why did he keep having to bring up the tension that had overrun their friendship since that damn kiss two years ago?

Because you want to push. Because you wish things were different.

Because you want her. And maybe you always have. Maybe it's always been her.

Goddamn his mind. Paul shook the thoughts from his head as he got out of the truck, following Abby up the porch steps and knocking on the door. There was barking, and then footsteps and the door swung open.

"Mr. Rice?" Paul asked.

He was a slight, wiry man with round glasses perched on the end of his nose and motor oil under his fingers. "That's right," he said. "Can I help you?"

"I'm Special Agent Paul Harrison," Paul said, flipping open his badge. "This is Abigail Winthrop, she's consulting with me today. We'd like to ask a few questions about your daughter, Keira."

Paul watched as the blood drained out of Morgan Rice's face. "Did you . . . did you find her?"

"No," Paul said gently. "But if you and your wife are willing to sit down with me, you might be able to help us."

"Of course, come in," Morgan said. "My wife's in town," he added. "Martha's got quilting circle on Wednesdays."

He ushered them into the house, where jute rugs and rough, natural wood furniture decorated the rooms. When they got to the living room, he gestured for them to sit on the couch.

Above the mantel, there was a picture of Keira, with two prayer candles with the Virgin of Guadalupe on them flanking the photo. The candles were lit, a rosary and some dried roses resting between them.

"So, what is this about?" Morgan asked.

"I'm investigating a case from fifteen years ago," Paul said. "In the process, I've found some similarities to Keira's case. And I wanted to speak to you about her."

"All right," Morgan said, and he could hear a hint of wariness in the man's voice.

"Keira went missing at a soccer meet in Yreka?"

"Yes," Morgan said. "Normally, my wife or I went with her. We'd chaperone. But my father was sick. So we thought it would be okay for her to go alone this one time." His lower lip wobbled, his eyes filling with tears. "It was a mistake," he whispered.

"Mr. Rice." Abby got up off the couch, grabbing the tissue box on the end table and gently pushing it into his hands. "Keira was sixteen. It was totally reasonable for you to let her go on a chaperoned field trip. This wasn't your mistake."

He grabbed one of the tissues, clutching it in his hand. "Keira is such a good girl," he said. "So talented."

Paul felt a growing pit in his stomach at the use of the present tense. This poor man. He could feel the loss in this house, the way it seemed to ache out of every wall. He remembered that feeling so well—that dull numb dread that was so damn hard to ignore.

If it was your child you lost, you can't ever ignore it.

"Mr. Rice, you said that you and your wife usually chaperoned," he said. "How long had Keira been playing soccer?"

"We had her in peewee soccer at five," he said. "Her coaches were talking scholarships when she was in middle school."

Paul could see Abby looking at him out of the corner of her eye, curious at this line of questioning. He wondered if all the other missing girls Zooey's Code Sibyl had picked out were soccer players. Was that how he was selecting his victims? Most of the Northern California teams in this part traveled up and down I-5 all the way to Oregon, to compete with other teams.

Was their unsub someone in the school system? A parent himself?

Paul couldn't discount any possibility. His work had taught him that even the most violent sociopath could have a family, people who loved him, people who had no idea what he was really like. Some of them were just that good at concealing who they really were.

"So sports are a big part of her life," Abby said. Paul noticed she had picked up on Morgan's use of the present tense, using it herself, so she wouldn't cause any ripples or offend.

"Oh, yeah," Morgan said. "All her friends play. When she went missing . . . her best friend, Jayden, she took it very hard. She was the one who was rooming with Keira that night. My wife and I tried to reassure her that it wasn't her fault, but it was very difficult for her."

Paul felt a twinge in his chest. Morgan Rice was clearly a good man. His concern for another child—his own missing child's best friend—made that clear. And the haunted look on Abby's face told him everything: that she was thinking about Cass, about the two of them. Of what she'd lost.

"Mr. Rice, do you mind if I use your bathroom?" Abby asked.

"Of course, it's just down the hall. Last door to the right."

"Thank you." Abby got up, shooting Paul a meaningful look. A look that clearly said, *distract him.*

What in the world was she up to? But he gave the slightest tilt of his head, to show he understood.

Abby disappeared down the hall, and Paul turned back to Morgan Rice, the questions mounting in his head.

CHAPTER 15

Teenage girls kept their secrets in two places: their rooms and their phones. Keira's phone was long since submitted as evidence, but when Abby opened the door across from the bathroom and peeked inside, she saw a laptop sitting on a blue-and-white painted desk.

Keira's desk was neat and orderly, and while everything was in the right place, there was no film of dust or stale air in here.

Her parents kept this room dusted and clean. The bed was made. Like they were waiting for her to come home.

Abby pressed a hand against her aching heart, trying to clear the sudden tightness in her throat. This was so sad. Morgan Rice looked like a shell of a man, tired and sad and running out of hope, fast. The little altar on the mantel, the dried flowers and rosary, had drawn her eye the moment he'd brought them into the living room. She hoped that their faith gave them some modicum of relief from the not-knowing.

She knew how terrible it was to wonder. But she had years of some kind of peace before that, before she realized that Wells hadn't killed Cass. She knew both sides of this coin: neither was good. They were just endured differently.

Keeping an ear out just in case Mr. Rice came looking to see why she was taking so long in the bathroom, Abby hurried over to the laptop on the desk and booted it up. She clicked on the messages icon, and bam, there they were: Keira's text messages.

She pulled a thumb drive out of her purse and pushed it into the USB slot, loading the messages—and the rest of the laptop—onto the drive, before plucking it out. She was about to shut the computer down, when she noticed the video chat icon on the dock was bouncing up and down.

Frowning, she clicked on it. And there it was: thousands of missed calls on Keira's Skype account. All from Keira's best friend, Jayden. Abby scrolled down, seeing that the calls went back nearly two years, ever since she went missing. They lessened after a while, but the most recent call had been last week.

That was some really heavy grief. Or . . . her

always curious mind thought, maybe some very heavy guilt?

She grabbed a pink, fluffy pen out of the cup on the desk and scribbled down Jayden's phone number and user name, dropping the piece of paper in her purse. She slipped out of the room, going across the hall to the bathroom and running the tap for a few seconds before going out again.

She smiled as she came into view of the living room and Paul got to his feet. His eyes were disapproving. He didn't like that she'd gone off and done some sleuthing on her own. *Control freak*, she thought, with more than a little affection.

"I think we've taken up enough of your time, Mr. Rice," Paul said, reaching out and shaking the man's hand. "Thank you for your time. I'll call you if I have any other questions."

Mr. Rice nodded. "Thank you for looking into Keira's disappearance," he said. "But, Agent Harrison? If you find my little girl? You call me first. I'll need to prepare her mother."

Abby had to bite the inside of her lip to keep from tearing up at the resigned look on Mr. Rice's face. He may talk about Keira like she was still alive, but he knew how slim that chance was, deep down. It was clear in his eyes.

"I promise, sir," Paul said solemnly.

"Thank you," Morgan said.

"Take care," Abby said, before she followed Paul out of the house.

He waited until they were back on the highway, headed home to Castella Rock, to say, "So, your snooping session turn anything up?"

Abby nodded at her purse, keeping her hands on the wheel as a semi merged in front of them. "Thumb drive in my purse. I loaded her entire laptop and all her texts onto it."

"You do realize this is completely illegal," Paul said, digging through her purse all the same.

"So arrest me," Abby dared. "I found out something useful."

"Oh?"

"Keira's Skype account was *full* of missed calls from her best friend. I'm talking thousands of calls over the last two years."

Paul frowned. "Why would she be calling Keira after she went missing?"

"You didn't call Cass's cell phone a few times, to hear her voice on the voice mail message?" Abby asked.

Silence fell in the cab of her truck, and she felt her stomach drop and embarrassed heat crawl up her chest and neck to flood her cheeks. "I guess it was just me," she muttered quickly.

"No, Winny, I—" He let out a long sigh, jerking

his hand through his hair, rumpling it. "I did," he admitted quietly. "Fuck, I must've played the videos I had of her a thousand times."

Her fingers were holding the steering wheel in a death grip. She tried to relax her fingers, but it was hard.

After Cass was killed, after Wells was caught, they'd had less than six months before graduating and going off to their separate colleges. They'd never sat down and talked about any of it as teenagers—they hadn't known how. And by the time they were adults, it was too late. They were supposed to have healed. Done their grieving and moved on.

She had tried. Maybe he had succeeded, until she dragged him back into this. She knew he'd been engaged to another FBI agent at some point. His mom had shown her pictures. His fiancée was a gorgeous woman, petite, but somehow beautifully fierce-looking. She didn't know what happened there, only that they never made it down the aisle and weren't together anymore.

But now he was back here, with her. And they had to talk about it, didn't they? Because she'd involved him in this.

Once again, Abby, you are the author of your own destruction, she thought.

"I think it might be more than that, though,"

Abby said. "Grief is one thing. But grief mixed with guilt? That's another."

"You think the best friend knows something?" Paul asked.

"You know how girls are at that age," Abby said. "They have entire secret lives from their parents. Even if they're close with them, like Keira Rice obviously was. But they don't keep secrets from their best friends."

You did. That traitorous thought floated to the surface, and she pushed it down. This wasn't the time.

"So you're just going to call her up and ask?" Paul asked.

"Why not?"

"It's not the worst idea," he said. His phone rang, and he looked down. "It's Zooey." He tapped it on. "Hey, Zo. You're on speaker with me and Abby."

"Great!" Zooey said. "I'm calling about the coroner's report."

"What about it?" Abby called.

"Well, it's not complete," Zooey said. "It looks like the FBI didn't do their own examination of the . . . of Cass's . . ." She hesitated. "Of Cass," she said finally. "They just relied on the county coroner's report. Problem is, both the copy in the FBI files I brought *and* the copy that Abby has in her files are missing pages."

"It's probably just a clerical error," Paul said.

"Probably," Zooey said. "But we should get the original just to be sure. Look, I don't mean to be an ass, but rural counties like this aren't exactly bastions of forensic progress. Add in the fact that we're talking fifteen years ago, which is practically the Dark Ages scientifically, there are things the ME might have missed that I'll be able to pick up."

"The original report would be at the sheriff's department, in the records room," Abby said to Paul.

"Okay, we'll dig around until I find it. And then"— he checked the time on his phone —"then, we all need to get ready for dinner. Because you're both invited to my mom's. No excuses."

"Ooh, Mama Harrison, I can't wait," Zooey said. "I'll see you in a bit."

"Hey, Zo, run some searches for me on the missing girls Code Sibyl pulled up," Paul said. "I want to know everything they had in common."

"On it," Zooey said.

"'Bye for now."

He hung up.

"It's probably best that you go to the sheriff's station alone," Abby said.

"Why's that?"

"Ryan's a deputy now."

"Ryan as in your ex-boyfriend from high school Ryan?" Paul asked.

Abby nodded. "When I moved back home to take care of Dad, he seemed to think it would be a good idea to pick things up again. That was about as far from my thinking as you could get. He didn't take it well."

"If I remember correctly, Ryan rarely takes anything well," Paul said.

"You can just drop me off at my place. Zooey and I can meet you at your mom's."

"Okay," he said. "I wouldn't let him bug you, though."

Abby shot him a look. "I can take care of myself when it comes to Ryan," she said. "I just don't feel like dealing with it today."

Once upon a time, breaking up with Ryan had been the peak of her teenage heartbreak. In fact, he had been the reason she and Cass had fought the day before Cass was killed.

Her throat tight as she pulled onto the road that led to her place, mind circling around those thousands of calls Jayden had made to Keira's Skype account. When the trees and the fence and the gate that had the wooden sign her father had carved himself, WINTHROP ACRES, affixed to it came into view, all the tension began to uncoil inside her. Home soothed her in a way little else did.

"I'll get out here," she said, when he pulled up to the gate.

"Abby, it's like half a mile down the road."

"I know, I need the fresh air."

He looked at her, searching, and the hair on the back of her arms stood on end under his scrutiny.

"We need to talk," he said. "About all this."

Abby bit her lip. She thought about what Zooey had told her, about the bomb, about the PTSD. She thought about the secrets she was still keeping. All the pain she kept hiding.

"I know," she said. "But not now."

She got out of the truck, leaving the keys behind for him. And he slid across the bench, taking her place in the driver's seat, waiting until she opened the gate and disappeared from sight, to drive away.

CHAPTER 16

Castella Rock, like many tiny rural towns, had a sheriff's department rather than a police department. When you had so many citizens living in the far-flung reaches of the county, a sheriff served the area better. Plus, the county never had money for both. It was always one or the other.

The sheriff's department was set in the town square. An old fountain was still spouting merrily, the cherubs' faces faded from years of water running over them, lending the whole thing a haunted air. The brick building the department operated out of was two stories, with a records room in the attic and a bell tower with a bell that hadn't rung in nearly fifty years.

Paul opened the glass doors, the brass handles worn from years and years of hands pulling them open. The building was cool and quiet this time of day, and when he walked into the main room, only one deputy was at his desk, his feet propped up as he looked intently at his phone.

Paul cleared his throat and the man started, looking up. When their eyes met, he felt a flash of recognition, followed quickly by disgust.

Ryan Clay. Abby's ex-boyfriend from high school . . . and his ex-rival on the baseball team. When Cass had been killed, Paul had quit the team, his focus shifting to law enforcement, college, and the FBI, and Ryan was finally number one. It was something that seemed to endlessly please him, because every time after that when he saw the guy, he'd talk loudly about all his wins and his new position as team captain.

Just looking at his face brought a rush of adolescent anger and annoyance to the surface, but Paul pushed it down. Hopefully, Ryan had just been a stupid egotistical kid who had changed. God knows, Paul had done and said some stupid shit as a teenager.

"Harrison," Ryan drawled, clearly trying to recover after being caught playing Candy Crush or whatever instead of working. "What are you doing here?"

Paul wasn't petty enough to flash his badge, so instead he just said, "I'm here on business. I need access to the records room."

Ryan's eyebrows scrunched together. "I don't think you're authorized to do that."

Clearly, the guy *hadn't* changed. "Is Sheriff Alan here?" he asked pointedly.

"Alan's on a call," Ryan said. "We've been dealing with an arsonist this entire fire season. Looks like we're finally gonna catch him."

"And they left you behind to watch the phones?" Paul asked innocently.

Ryan's mouth flattened. "You're going to have to come back later," he said firmly. "Maybe with a warrant."

Paul sighed, pulling out his phone. He dialed a number, raising the phone to his ear. "Hi, Sheriff," he said, when Alan picked up. "It's Paul Harrison."

"Paul!" Sheriff Alan, who'd been the sheriff ever since Baker retired after Cass's murder, was a jovial man who looked like he belonged in a Santa suit more than with a sheriff's badge. He was also a dedicated, loyal public servant with a keen mind. "Son of a gun, I heard you were in town for your daddy's memorial. I'm so sorry I wasn't able to make it, but Nancy said she had a nice talk with your momma. How are you?"

"I'm good, Alan," Paul said. "Listen, I'm actually at the department right now. I need access to the records room. There's a cold case I'm looking into."

There was a pause, a weighted one, as Alan absorbed this information. "You looking into what I think you are?" he asked.

Paul owed Alan a lot. When he graduated college, his grades were just barely enough to get him into Quantico. He'd never been good at tests, and that hurt him in the long run. But Alan had not only written him a recommendation, he'd gotten several of his high-connected law enforcement friends—and a politician—in Sacramento to write ones as well. Paul was pretty sure those letters were the reason he got into Quantico, where he was able to flourish and show what he was truly capable of.

"Some new details have come to light," Paul said. "I need to investigate."

Alan sighed. "I respect you too much to tell you no," he said. "Plus, you could just make a few calls and get them yourself. Is it Clay who's giving you a problem?"

"That's right," Paul said.

"Put me on speaker," Alan said.

Paul hit the button on his phone. "There you go, Alan."

"Clay!" Sheriff Alan barked, his voice changing from jovial to drill sergeant in one syllable.

"Pull your head out of your ass and give Harrison access to the records room. The man's FBI, for God's sake!"

A humiliated flush rose on Ryan's cheeks. "Yes sir," he ground out.

"Thanks, Alan," Paul said, turning the speaker off. "Hope to see you before I leave town."

"Keep me in the loop if you find something," Alan said. "My boys are at your disposal once they catch this firebug."

"Good luck with that. I'll let you go," Paul said. "'Bye now."

"See ya, Harrison," Alan replied, hanging up.

As soon as his boss wasn't on the line, Ryan snarled, "You think you're some big deal, don't you, Harrison?"

Paul raised an eyebrow. "Ryan, I just want access to the case files. If you haven't left the petty shit behind in high school like I did, that's your problem. Records room still in the same place?"

Ryan nodded brusquely. "Access code is 5432."

"Thanks," Paul said. "I'll be leaving you to your very important work now." The sarcasm dripped off his voice as he turned to leave the office and head up to the records room.

"Tell Abby I said hi," Ryan said pointedly.

Paul stopped, knowing he was giving the

guy the exact reaction he wanted. But then he turned, a wolfish smile on his face, all teeth and edge and warning. "I'm betting Abby wouldn't like that," he said.

"Abby doesn't like a lot of things that are good for her," Ryan said. "It's the way women are."

"How's that misogynistic worldview working for you?" Paul asked, disgusted, and Ryan's lips curled in a sneer as he shifted from foot to foot like a boxer prepping for a match.

The tension in the room made Paul feel like he was walking on a razor wire. Guys like Ryan were pretty predictable—unless they snapped.

And he remembered all too well the one time he witnessed Ryan snapping. Because when he was still playing baseball, he'd been the one to restrain Ryan from nearly killing some kid on the rival team. Paul had come on the field just as Ryan had started kicking the guy's head in with his cleats—if Paul hadn't dragged him away, there would've been permanent damage. After that, Paul had watched him like a hawk whenever Ryan was with Abby, worried that his explosive temper would someday be directed at her.

When they broke up, Paul had been relieved, even though Abby had seemed heartbroken. But just a month later, Cass was killed, and all thoughts about Ryan Clay and the possible threat he posed had fled Paul's mind.

He wasn't intimidated by this guy even though he knew what his type was capable of. Because he knew exactly what *he* was capable of, and Ryan wasn't even on the same stratosphere.

Paul wasn't the type to throw his power around. Why would he? People looked at him and saw a tall, affable guy who they wanted to trust. It came in damn useful in his line of work.

But he'd spent almost twenty years training in various martial arts. It was one of the reasons it still killed him that Mancuso had gotten the better of him in the Thebes case. He should've been able to adapt in that moment, but he hadn't, because his concern for his team had distracted him.

It was a hard lesson to learn. But he was man enough to learn it.

Without another word, Paul just turned and left the office, heading upstairs. He was halfway up to the third floor when he heard footsteps behind him.

God, was the asshole really following him? Paul didn't turn back, he just reached the top floor and walked over to the records room door, punching in the code and opening it. File cabinets lined the walls, with evidence boxes on

free-standing shelves in the middle of the room.
Paul flipped on the lights, and they flickered a
few times before finally beaming bright.

"What are you looking for, anyway?" Ryan
asked, coming up behind him.

"It's need-to-know," Paul said, heading over
to the filing cabinet marked *M*. He turned to
look at Ryan. "I'm good on my own."

Ryan folded his arms across his chest, his chin
tilting up. "I've got more right to be here than
you, Harrison."

Paul rolled his eyes, jerking open the filing cabinet. "Fine. Stand there like an ass." He
leafed through the files in the cabinet, pulling
out the thick one labeled MARTIN, CASSAN-
DRA. He set it on top of the cabinet, noting the
case number, and then going over to the shelf,
where the evidence boxes were. But the box
with Cass's case number on it wasn't there.

"Where do you guys store the evidence for
closed cases?" Paul asked.

"Basement," Ryan said.

Paul checked the time on his phone. It was too
late to grub through the basement today and
make it to dinner on time. He'd already can-
celed lunch on his mom, so there'd be hell to
pay if he didn't show for dinner with Abby and
Zooey in tow.

"Okay. I guess I'll be back tomorrow, then." He grabbed the case file, tucking it under his arm, and walked past Ryan, who was still standing there like he thought he was some sort of guard of the records room.

God, that guy was a piece of work, Paul thought as he made his way out of the sheriff's station and back to his mother's house. The sun was starting to dip in the sky, and the wind chimes on the porch tinkled and danced in the breeze as he parked Abby's truck and got out.

"Hey, stranger," called Rose, his youngest sister, from the porch swing. "You keep disappearing on us."

"Abby wanted me to do something for her," he said, smiling and walking up to sit next to her.

"Oh, really, now?" Rose asked.

"It's not like that," he said. Were all his sisters going to give him a hard time about Abby tonight? Probably. They clearly were gearing up for their torture-our-only-brother time.

Rose was the daughter most like their mother. She had eschewed traditional college and instead had thrown herself full tilt into orchard management, a farm girl through and through. Paul didn't think Rose would ever want to leave Castella Rock.

There was one in each generation. The one to

take up the mantle of this land that had been in their family for so long. Rose was the one. Paul was thankful, because he and his other sisters—even Faye, with all her hands-on business sense—weren't suited for it.

Rose was the shortest in the family, barely topping five feet. *All the height was used up before we got to you, sweetheart, I'm sorry*, his dad used to say with a laugh. Her blond hair was like corn silk, and her little nose was always just a bit pink, because she forgot to wear her hat while working in the orchard.

"Faye and Georgia inside?" he asked.

"Mom's making meatballs," Rose said. "And Mara Skyped in. You missed it."

Their middle sister, Mara, was currently overseas working with Doctors without Borders. An OB/GYN, she provided vital maternal care in war-torn countries, which meant she'd missed almost as many family events as Paul had, something the two of them had bonded about through the years.

"Is that Paul?" Georgia peeked her head out of the screen door. "Faye! Paul's here!"

There was the sound of skipping footsteps, and Faye, his bombastic, wild, ready-for-anything sister came bounding out. Her blond hair was piled on top of her head haphazardly, and she was wearing an apron that said KISS THE COOK.

"Finally," Faye said. "What took you so long?"

"Abby," Rose replied.

"Ah," Faye said knowingly.

"It's always Abby, isn't it?" Georgia asked with a pointed grin.

"All of you, stop," Paul said. "Abby is a friend. And she is going to be here in about ten minutes *with* one of my colleagues from work, so please don't embarrass me."

His sisters all blinked innocently at him, and Rose got up to stand next to her sisters, linking arms with them as they smiled at him. "Us?" Georgia batted her eyes.

"Embarrass you?" Faye said.

"We'd never!" Rose added.

Oh, God. He was so doomed. Why had he let his mother talk him into this when he called to cancel lunch?

"Oh, look, there they are!" Georgia called out, looking over his shoulder.

Paul turned, to see Zooey and Abby making their way up the drive. Abby spotted them and waved. She was holding something in her hands—it looked like banana bread. How she'd managed to pull that together in the time it took him to get Cass's case file, he had no idea.

Abby always had a certain kind of capable magic about her. Maybe it was because she'd grown up without a mom; she'd kind of been forced to mother herself.

"Abby!" Rose bounded down the steps, hugging her. Paul hadn't realized the two had grown close, but he guessed it made sense. Abby had an entire orchard on her hands now, and Rose did more and more of the day-to-day work for their mom these days. The two probably had a lot in common now.

"You must be Zooey," said Georgia with a warm smile when the women made their way up the steps. "It's *so* nice to meet you."

"Seriously, we never get to meet Paul's co-workers," Faye said. "I'm Faye. This is Georgia. And Rose."

"It's nice to meet all of you," Zooey said. "I've heard a lot about all of you."

"You better not be tellin' stories about us," Georgia scolded Paul.

"All good things," Zooey reassured her, winking at Paul.

"Now I know she's lying," Faye joked, drawing Zooey inside the orchard house.

His mother had always prided herself on making a warm home—and she'd always succeeded. Filled with light and with art—a potpourri from a local artist, drawings by each of her children when they were little, and even a few prints of her favorite fairy tales—it was a bright, cheerful home with old, creaky wood floors and seven different ways of sneaking out, if you were clever and quiet.

"You must tell us why you're here," Faye was saying to Zooey.

"It's business, Faye," Paul said warningly.

Faye rolled her eyes. "Next thing you know, you're gonna be all, 'It's classified, Faye.'" She lowered her voice in a mimicry of Paul's, making the rest of her sisters and Zooey laugh.

"Hey." Paul grabbed Abby's hand as his sisters brought Zooey into the kitchen to introduce her to their mother. He tugged her into the space under the stairs, where it was quiet and secluded. "I got the file."

"Did you check the ME's report for the missing pages?" she asked.

He shook his head. "Not yet. But the evidence from the case, it wasn't in the records room. I'm gonna have to go tomorrow and get it out of the basement."

Her eyes widened. "You think Sheriff Alan will let us have it?"

"Yeah," he said. "Clay was there, by the way. Christ, that guy's grown into an even bigger ass since I last saw him."

Abby sighed. "Yeah, I know. Ever since Georgia beat his dad in the mayor's race, he's gotten an even bigger chip on his shoulder. I think that's one of the reasons he joined the department. He wanted to feel like a big man again."

"That's the worst reason to join law enforcement," Paul said, disgusted. "It's dangerous."

"I know," Abby said. "But it is what it is. I don't think Ryan's actually a risk to anyone. He's just a jerk."

Paul didn't want to tell her about how Ryan had steered the conversation toward her. She didn't need that on her mind—not with everything else happening. "We can go over the file after dinner at your place," he said as his mother called, "Abby? Paul? Where are you two?"

"Coming, Mom!" he said.

He looked down, realizing he was still holding Abby's hand, and he let go, feeling a strange sense of loss when he did. He cleared his throat. "We should go."

"Yeah," Abby said. She licked her lips, and his eyes darted to the spot, unable to look away for a moment. "Meatballs await."

CHAPTER 17

My dear Paeon,

Another two years have passed. Doesn't time fly?

Or maybe it doesn't, for you. Apologies. There I go again, making the mistake of thinking we are the same.

The years have made it very clear we aren't. After all, you are who you are. And I am who I am.

The Harvest is coming. Can you feel it? So much fruit, ripe on the vine, ready for the picking. The choices are dizzying. The array bright and beautiful and endless in its possibilities.

And it's all mine.

Does that rankle you? That your student outpaced you in every way? You rot in there, while I'm out here, with the harvest to myself.

You should have listened.

You should have learned.
Have you learned, dear friend?
Or must I teach you another lesson?

                  Yours, sincerely,

                  Antaeus

CHAPTER 18

Antaeus—

A sweet little fox visited last week. I sent her your way.

Happy hunting, my young pupil.

This time, the lesson to be learned is yours.

—Paeon

CHAPTER 19

The next morning, Abby, Zooey, and Paul met at the Winthrop farmhouse to pore over the ME's report. But their triumph at securing the original file was short-lived.

"This is the same exact one with the missing pages," Zooey said in frustration, tossing the file on the desk.

Paul frowned. "Files get moved, things get lost. You know how it is."

"I want to talk to the ME," Zooey said. "This . . ." She leaned over to look at the report. "Dr. August Jeffrey. Is he still the ME?"

"Yep," Abby said. "He's where I got my version of the file."

"Okay, so he's friendly," Zooey said, looking hopefully at Paul. "I need to know all the facts here, Paul, in order to discover anything science-wise. There could have been forensic evidence they didn't have the money to test. The FBI took over so fast, things could've got lost in communication. There's a million reasons things can get overlooked on a rural case like this, so why not go straight to the source?"

"I can take her to talk to Dr. Jeffrey while you search the basement for the evidence boxes," Abby offered.

"Okay," Paul said. "It's a plan."

"You ready now?" Abby asked Zooey.

She nodded, getting out of the chair and grabbing her bag, slinging it over her shoulders.

"Good luck at the sheriff's station, boss," she said.

"Feed Roscoe for me, will you?" Abby asked.

"You're always trying to get me to do your chores, Winny," he said, with a roguish smile that made her stomach twist.

"Thank you," she said pointedly. "See you later."

"So give me the rundown on the ME. What's he like?" Zooey asked after they'd loaded up into Abby's truck and merged onto the highway.

"Dr. Jeffrey is in his seventies now," Abby said as she let a red sports car that clearly had *very important* places to be pass her. "He was the county ME since the sixties. He's an institution."

"Did he seem shady during his interview?"

Abby shook her head. "Nothing really leapt

out at me when we talked. But I didn't even realize there were pages missing from the ME's report, so maybe I just missed it. Over the course of the last year, I talked to Dr. Jeffrey, Sheriff Alan, who was just a deputy on the case at the time, and several of the other deputies who worked the case before the FBI took over."

"I was looking over who was in charge on the FBI side," Zooey said, flipping open the thick file she had in her lap. "It was an Agent Barson, who was kind of infamous at the Bureau."

Abby frowned. "Infamous how?"

"Well, Barson was a really good agent when he started. But he also developed a *really* big cocaine problem."

"Oh, God," Abby said.

"Yeah," Zooey said. "And he rode on the 'I caught Dr. X' wave for a while, so he didn't get caught and fired until 2005. There was a whole internal investigation and then *another* one when Director Edenhurst took over. They re-examined several of his cases, but I guess this one didn't ring any alarm bells, since Howard Wells confessed." She paused, frowning out the window for a second. "I don't get why he confessed," she said. "Even if your theory that they met online is right, and he doesn't know who our unsub was, why would he confess?

Why not try to wriggle out of it? The forensic evidence alone could have *maybe* clinched it for a jury, but maybe not. Juries get frustrated when you talk too much science at them. And Wells is charismatic—he could have weaseled his way out of it."

"He'd never be able to kill that way again, though," Abby said softly. "He couldn't perform his whole ritual. The strangulation, the marking of his victims. He would've had to change."

"You think he confessed so he could keep his killing MO intact?" Zooey asked, sounding skeptical.

Abby shrugged. "You're probably more of an expert on serial killers than I am," she said. "But I've talked to everyone I could who knew Wells, and so much of what they told me was the same: He was a control freak, he had to have things *just* his way. One of his scrub nurses from his surgery days told me a story about how she would have to use a ruler to measure exactly one and three-eighths inches between his surgical tools on the tray, because anything less or more, he'd notice, and freak out."

"We are dealing with an *enormous* ego," Zooey said thoughtfully. "I mean, just with the surgeon factor—you have to have supreme self-confidence to be a successful one. But if he was ruled by ego, why did he quit surgery to go work in a morgue in the middle of nowhere?"

That was a good point. "Something must have happened," Abby said. "What do you guys call it? A triggering incident?"

Zooey nodded as Abby pulled off the highway, taking the exit into town.

Castella Rock was the kind of town that had stop signs—and no stop lights. Only about 5,000 people lived in the town proper, most of the citizens living outside the town, on farms, orchards, and small ranches. Main Street split the town in two, with three streets on the east side of town, three streets on the west side. And not much south or north but farmland. There was one gas station, two churches, a tiny library that was more a labor of love than anything, and the school, which had gotten a fresh coat of paint this summer. Problem was, the strapped one-school district had bought the paint on discount, so now the school was painted an ugly, dirty-looking brick red.

Dr. Jeffrey lived with his wife, Mamie, in a sweet little white house with green shutters on Marigold Street. He was waiting for the two of them on the porch, sitting in the antique 1920s glider, leaning against pillows Mamie stitched herself.

"Howdy, girls." He tipped his cowboy hat, gesturing for them to take a seat in the chairs across the glider. "Iced tea?"

"Please," Zooey said.

"Thank you for taking the time to see us," Abby said. "I know it was sort of last minute."

"Oh, come now, this old man is happy for the company."

"Well, you know I've been working on a book," Abby said. "About Cass."

Dr. Jeffrey nodded. "I think it's a very nice way to honor her, Abby."

Abby smiled. "Thank you. I hope so too. But you know me, I like having all the research in front of me."

"I remember all your note cards," he said with a grin.

"Exactly," Abby said. "Zooey here, she's got some STEM field experience in forensics and such." She didn't want to scare Dr. Jeffrey off by saying Zooey was with the FBI. "She's been helping me figure out all the medical and science jargon," she said, with a disarming smile, going full sweet country girl on him. "Anyway, Zooey is cataloging stuff for me, making notes, you know. And she noticed that there are a few pages missing from Cass's autopsy report. I thought it was a mistake or something, but when I went

looking for the original at the sheriff's department, the same pages were missing."

Dr. Jeffrey set his iced tea on the table. "Oh,
you know how things get, over the years," he
said. "Sheriff Alan's probably had to move those
records in and out of the upstairs a dozen times
because of that leaky roof. I'm sure those pages
just got lost in the shuffle."

He looked at his watch. "You know, Mamie's
gonna need me to pick her up from bingo soon."

"Bingo doesn't even start until noon," Abby
said, frowning, and the good doctor's cheeks
reddened at being caught in his lie. "August,"
she said, her voice lowering in her seriousness.
"What are you not telling me here?"

"Abigail," he said, and it was more of a warning than anything. It sent chills down her arms.
"You're a sweet girl. A good girl. A talented girl.
You don't need to put tawdry details that'll get
a lot of people hurt in your book about Cass."

A horrible prickling feeling spread from the
bottom of her spine to the top. "Tawdry details?
What are you talking about?"

Next to her, she saw Zooey bite her lip.

"Sir?" Zooey asked the doctor. "Was she pregnant? Is that why the pages are missing?"

Dr. Jeffrey didn't need to say anything. The
proof was written all over his face.

Spots danced along the edge of her vision as her ears roared. *Pregnant?* No! Cass would have told her. She would've confided in her.

Would she have really, after what Ryan told her? that horrible voice in the back of her head asked.

Her fingers clenched around the arms of the wooden rocking chair, her mind racing. Cass had been gone for almost a month the summer she died, visiting her grandma. They were supposed to get coffee the day after she got back. Cass had cancelled on her, and considering the fight they'd had before she left, Abby couldn't exactly blame her.

"How far along was she?" Zooey asked.

"Three months at least," Dr. Jeffrey said.

Three months. She might've known during their fight. Oh, God . . . that meant . . .

Paul.

Abby felt the bottom drop out of her stomach. Paul hadn't just lost Abby that night. He'd lost his *child*. A child he hadn't even known existed.

"August, why in the world did you keep this secret?" she demanded. "You hindered two investigations—the sheriff's and the FBI's."

"I kind of want to know that too," Zooey said. "Because this is vital information the FBI wasn't given."

"It was Sheriff Baker who told me to bury it,"

Dr. Jeffrey said. "I brought my results to him first. And he told me I had to keep it quiet. That it would break Cassandra's mother's heart."

Abby's frown deepened. Maryann Martin was a lot of things, but she was a strong woman, she'd survived Cass's murder. She would've survived this. She felt angry on Maryann's behalf, that these men had decided that they knew better than her. That they understood her strength more than her.

"Well, that's some good ol' boy bullshit right there," Zooey declared. "You took that woman's right to grieve away. You withheld an important fact from law enforcement. You didn't do the right thing, sir. And as a doctor, as a scientist, I would think you would understand how people like me need the *full picture* to do our job. To catch the killers."

"I don't understand why you're so upset," Dr. Jeffrey said, his eyes wide. "I understand this news is a shock, Abby. But holding back the news of Cass's pregnancy didn't hinder *anything*. Her killer is behind bars."

Abby took a deep breath. "It was a copycat, August."

All the color drained from the man's wrinkled cheeks. "What?"

"Cass's killer, he killed her to frame Howard Wells. He made it look like Wells's killing method. Cass's killer is still free."

"And we think he's still active," Zooey said. "That he's been active for the last sixteen years. So it's time to dig deep, Doc. Please tell me you saved the pages from the medical report."

He sighed. "I gave them to Sheriff Baker," he said.

"And where's he?" Zooey asked.

"He died five years ago," Abby said.

Zooey pursed her lips, breathing hard through her nose. "Okay. Okay. Then we're going to get creative. Doc? You're gonna go in that sweet little house of yours, pull out a notebook, and you're going to write down every thing you remember from the autopsy and medical report. I'm gonna pick it up later on tonight and we're going to talk over everything you remember."

"You're very impertinent, young lady," he said.

"And you obstructed an FBI investigation," Zooey said. "The sweet little old man act won't work on me. Like you said, I'm impertinent. Abby?"

Abby got up. She still felt numb, like she was walking through cement. "I'm sorry, August," she said, not really knowing why *she* was doing the apologizing. He'd known this this whole time. He'd known this when she came to him for the copy of the exam. And he thought a promise to another man was more important than her uncovering the truth. Because he was an old-school guy who thought that a teen pregnancy would somehow taint Cass's memory.

Maybe in the eyes of men like him. But not Abby's. And certainly not Mrs. Martin's.

Abby felt a twinge of pain at the thought of Cass's mother as she and Zooey headed down the street, where her truck was parked. She needed to go see Maryann. It'd been a few months since she'd checked in.

In a way, she was just as bad as Dr. Jeffrey and Sheriff Baker. She'd kept the truth from Mary-ann too.

You didn't know for sure until now, she thought. It was her one saving grace. But she needed to go tell her. And soon.

"You look like you need a drink," Zooey declared as they came to a stop in front of her truck.

"It's not even noon yet," she said.

"Okay, good point," Zooey said. "French fries it is."

Without another word, the younger woman plucked the keys out of Abby's hand and climbed into the driver's seat of her truck. Abby got in the driver's seat, letting Zooey drive them to The Pit, Castella Rock's best—and only—diner.

They took a red vinyl booth in the back, and Abby leaned her head in her palms as Zooey ordered fries and two chocolate shakes.

"You knew," Abby said finally, after their food came and Zooey poured about half the shaker of salt on her own plate of fries. "Even before he started acting suspicious. You knew she was pregnant."

"I had my suspicions," Zooey said. "The pages of the report that were missing were the ones that would've detailed a pregnancy. I didn't want to say it, just in case I was wrong. My hunches aren't always right. I'm more of a science girl."

Abby stared at her plate of fries. "I can't believe I didn't know," she said. "I can't believe she didn't tell me."

"Maybe she'd just found out. Maybe she needed more time. This isn't your fault, Abby."

But maybe it was. Maybe, if she and Cass had met for coffee that day like they were supposed to, she would've never crossed paths with that sick psychopath. Maybe she'd be sitting across from her right now, the mother of a fifteen-year-old.

God. Abby felt sick. She ran her hands through

her hair, trying to breathe deep and gain some kind of control. She needed to get herself together.

She was going to have to tell Paul.

"I don't know how to tell him this."

Zooey sighed, plucking the paper off her straw and sticking it in her shake. "Yeah . . . this is really messed up," she said. "It's going to be really hard."

"He's going to be devastated," Abby said, shaking her head, bewildered and overwhelmed.

"There's a lot of history here for both of you," Zooey said.

"We're all tangled up in each other," Abby admitted, softly, a confessional she had to get off her chest. She felt like she was losing grasp of everything—her emotions, her heart, her words—as she just kept talking. "Sometimes I think it's my fault."

"What's your fault?" Zooey asked, her black brows drawing together. "Cass's murder? That's ridiculous, Abby. Look at all you've done to find her real killer, when no one else was even thinking they had to look."

"You didn't know me back then," Abby said. "Cass and I . . . we were always so close. But that summer she was killed, it was like things were falling apart. *We* were falling apart."

"What happened?" Zooey asked. "Did you guys have a fight?"

"The fight to end all fights," Abby said. "My high school boyfriend dumped me at the end of the school year, and at first, Cass was supportive. And then she started getting really distant. The night before she left for her grandmother's for a month, I finally got the nerve up to confront her about it."

"What did she say?"

Abby could still feel the tightness in her chest, how her cheeks had flooded with heat, when the words had spilled out of Cass's mouth: *Ryan says he dumped you because you're after Paul.*

"She said that at first, she waved Ryan's concerns off," she told Zooey. "She thought he was just bitter. But then she started really thinking about it. And that she'd decided that Paul and I were way too close. That he was way too concerned about me when Ryan dumped me. That she'd let it go on for way too long. That things needed to change."

Abby stared at her hands. "I admit it, I was pissed at her. It felt like she was accusing me of something. Other than Cass, Paul was my best friend. And I spent the next four weeks being mad and petty and I didn't avoid Paul at all. Sometimes teen girls can be vicious, and I was.

I spent as much time with him as possible. Doing all our normal summer stuff. So when Cass came back, she cancelled on me when we were supposed to get coffee. And so the next time I saw her, she was in a coffin."

"Abby, I'm so sorry," Zooey said. "I had no idea."

"No one does," Abby said. "And now . . ." She let out a sharp, bitter laugh. "Now I'm sitting here wondering if she was telling me to back off not just her man—but her baby-daddy. And I'm sixteen years removed from it now, I'm older now, and I'm wondering if she had a damn point."

"You mean you had feelings for Paul back then," Zooey said.

"I don't know," Abby said, feeling hopeless and guilty and just so damn sad for the girl Cass had been, the girl she had been, the woman she got to be, while Cass never had the chance.

Paul had been her home and history and heart for so long, maybe he'd never left. Maybe he'd always been there.

"Nothing ever happened back then," Abby stressed. "I'd never do that to Cass. And neither would he. But he's my childhood. He's the boy next door. I was seventeen, and then my entire world blew up and I lost one of the most important people to me. And all I could think, after, was that maybe she died hating me. So whatever there was there, if there was anything between him and me, I just denied it."

But now . . .

Oh, but now.

She couldn't let herself go there. Not after the line she'd drawn in the sand two years ago, her on one side, him on the other, never, ever to cross.

"I'm sorry," Abby said suddenly, jerking up, realizing she was spilling her entire heart out to one of Paul's co-workers. She turned positively scarlet at the thought. "I shouldn't have . . . you don't need me dumping all this on you."

"It's fine," Zooey said. "I have one of those faces. People tend to tell me stuff. It's what made me such a good criminal."

Abby blinked, momentarily distracted from her own problems by this revelation. "You were a criminal?"

Zooey nodded. "Remember how I said Paul saved me? I wasn't kidding. He just kind of saved me from myself.

"I was in foster care from an early age," Zooey explained. "No one really cared about me. I ran away, when I was fourteen. I started out stealing cars. The new ones are basically rolling computers, so if you've got a hacker's skill . . ." She shrugged. "I made enough money for college that way. Dodged the system—or really, hacked it—until I aged out. Went to MIT. Dropped out. I thought I'd go back to boosting cars, but I ended up on someone's radar. Someone really bad."

"Who?"

"A bombmaker," Zooey said. "I have a bit of a knack with chemistry. And this guy? He was all about chemical weapons. Sold them on the black market all over the world. Didn't matter what fascist government wanted them—as long as the price was right, he'd make the sale. He decided that I was going to be his newest apprentice. Whether I wanted to be or not."

"Holy crap," Abby said.

"Yeah," Zooey said. "I was lucky. I had a window of time to 'make the right choice,' as he put it. Twenty-four hours. So I got on a train to DC and I stood outside FBI headquarters and I hacked into their servers, right outside their doors."

"What?" Abby was agog. Why in the world would she do that? How was she standing here right now, if she could do that?

"I didn't do any damage," Zooey assured her. "I just sent one message: 'I'm outside.' And they came running. Armed to the teeth, of course, and that was kind of freaky, but they brought me inside pretty fast. Cuffed, of course."

"Zooey, you . . . that's the most reckless plan I've ever heard in my life," Abby said, a little awed at her gumption. "You did it to prove how valuable you could be to the FBI, right?"

Zooey grinned. "I knew you were smart," she said. "Exactly. If I had just walked in, seeking sanctuary, babbling about an international dealer in chemical weapons with no real concrete proof, they'd probably throw me out. And then he'd get me. I had to prove my worth. Right away. The boss—and Agent Sinclair—were the ones to do my initial interview."

Abby frowned. "How old were you?"

"Nineteen," Zooey said. "Paul fought for me. The director at the time thought I'd be a security risk. But Paul got me to Quantico for the training I needed. I even teach a course there on poisons now."

"Wow," Abby said. "You've come totally full circle. That's amazing."

"I don't tell you this to brag," Zooey said. "I'm telling you this because I want you to know I understand, what it's like to be on the outside looking in. For a lot of my life, that's how I felt. Until I walked into FBI headquarters. Which is pretty ironic considering how I spent most of my teenage years."

"Thank you," Abby said. "I appreciate it, especially after I dumped all my emotions on you."

"Like I said, I have one of those faces," Zooey said as the waitress dropped off the check.

"So, what happened?" Abby asked. "With the bombmaker?"

Zooey's lips tightened, her normal cheerful countenance seeming to flicker for a moment. "He's still out there," she said quietly. "They've never been able to track him down. But someday . . . I'm going to. He and I have business to settle."

Abby understood this. She recognized the steely glint in Zooey's eyes.

It's how she felt about Cass's killer. About the specter of death that had been haunting Northern California, no one the wiser, because he was a little more clever than most.

She had business to settle with him. The kind of business that involved him looking down the barrel of her Winchester.

And she'd be damned if anyone stopped her.

CHAPTER 20

By the time Paul had eaten breakfast with his family and helped his mother fix a beam in the barn, it was nearly noon. He sped a little down the highway on his way to the courthouse, where the evidence boxes from Cass's case—the ones the FBI had deemed nonessential—would be.

He wasn't feeling very hopeful that he'd find the missing pages of the medical report there, but he'd try for Zooey. If she thought there might be missing forensic evidence, finding the missing pages was a lot better than the alternative.

Because the alternative involved things like exhuming bodies. His stomach clenched at the thought.

He wasn't going to do that. Or let Zooey do that. He knew she wouldn't even bring it up unless it was her only, last resort, but he prayed he'd find the damn missing pages so he didn't even have to think about it.

The courthouse was an old Art Deco building from the 1930s that was the only place in town that had a basement. He checked himself in at the front, walking through the metal detector that looked like it was from the seventies. The security guard raised an eyebrow at his badge.

"This real?" he asked.

"It is indeed," Paul said. "Do you mind?"

He took the badge back from the man, tucking it in his back pocket. It felt awkward there. He spent most of his days in a suit, his badge tucked in the inside jacket pocket. But he was in jeans and flannel and cowboy boots today, and he felt oddly off balance, suddenly.

Did he even belong here anymore? Had he ever?

He took the elevator down to the basement, smiling at the dark-haired older woman sitting behind the desk in front of the evidence locker. A long line of chain-link fence was strung behind her, and Paul couldn't blame the sheriff for beefing up security—there were a lot more drug confiscations around these parts with the rise of heroin and meth. Sometimes, an addict could get so reckless that even the idea of robbing the law seemed like a good idea.

"Hi there," Paul said, glancing at the little name placard that said *Annie Wheeler*. "Annie, I'm Special Agent Paul Harrison, FBI. I believe Sheriff Alan called and said I'd be coming by?"

The woman's face broke into a wide smile. She was round and soft and cute, her curly dark hair springing up around her head like a middle-aged Betty Boop. "You're Tandy's boy!"

"I am," he said.

"Your mother is so proud of you," she said. "All she does is talk about you. We ran the Christmas Fair at the church last year together, and it was the best year ever. We raised over five thousand dollars for the homeless shelter."

"That's great," Paul said.

"But Sheriff Alan did call and give me a heads-up you'd be coming," Annie said, getting up and fishing a large ring of keys out of her desk. "He told me to let you wander around, take whatever you wanted." She unlocked the chain on the gate into the evidence locker, pulling it open. "I do have to lock it behind you, though. Sheriff Alan brought in a bunch of heroin this morning. They were looking for that arsonist and instead came across a whole operation in a warehouse outside of town. Can you imagine? What are people thinking these days, I swear. They need the good Lord to guide them."

"I'm sorry Alan's having such trouble with that arsonist," Paul said.

"Four fires now," Annie said, tutting. "Like the world's not burning down fast enough already. Anyway, you go on, find what you need. I'll be right here when you're ready."

"Thanks, Annie," Paul said.

The evidence locker was dimly lit by a lone bulb that swung back and forth with the vibrations from the movement upstairs in the courthouse. Paul scanned the shelves and the neatly labeled brown boxes, trying to get a sense of how they were organized. It didn't seem to be completely chronological, and it took him a few moments to realize the sheriff had organized the place by crime and *then* alphabetized the sections.

"Okay, homicide," Paul muttered to himself, scanning the boxes. His eyes lighted on the name *EVANS, CASEY*. He knew that name. It was the football player who had drowned over Labor Day weekend Paul's freshman year. Foul play had been suspected, but there'd never been enough evidence. He was in the right section, at least.

He spent the next fifteen minutes going through the boxes in the homicide section. And then, when he couldn't find any of them with

Cass's name or her case number, he began to go through the entire room.

An hour later, he'd checked every single evidence box.

Cass's weren't here.

"Hey, Annie," he called.

"Yeah, Paul?" she asked, hurrying over and unlocking the gate and letting him out. "You find what you need?"

He shook his head. "You keep a log, right? Of who checks out what evidence?"

"Sure," Annie said. "It's right here." She went over to her desk and pulled out a logbook, handing it over to him.

Paul's stomach clenched as he saw the last entry, made this morning.

Ryan Clay, checking out Case #543

Paul felt a curl of disgust in his stomach. What was this guy's problem? He must've snooped to see what file Paul was looking for in the records room yesterday and decided to fuck with him.

His fists clenched and he tried to breathe deeply. This was the kind of petty bullshit he hated. He wasn't someone who played games. And Ryan seemed determined to do some stupid, pointless male posturing to make himself feel better when all it was going to do was get his ass handed to him—first by Paul, then by his boss.

"Thanks, Annie," he said. "You've been a great help."

She blushed. "Tell your mom I said hi."

"Will do. 'Bye now."

He headed out of the courthouse, blinking in the sudden sunlight after being in the dim basement for the last hour. He put in a call to Sheriff Alan, but it went to voice mail. He didn't want to leave a message chewing out the man's deputy, so he decided he'd track down Ryan's address and go there himself.

But first, he needed to stop by the farmhouse and see if Abby and Zooey had made any progress on the Dr. Jeffrey front.

As he drove down Orchard Row, the windows rolled down, the cooling autumn air filling his lungs, he found himself thinking about Abby.

And thinking about Abby always led him to think about regrets. He didn't regret much in his life—he tried hard not to, even with how he and his fiancée had ended their engagement—but most of his regrets were centered around the two girls who had shaped him more than anyone else.

That month before Cass was killed had been

confusing for him. She'd been up visiting her grandmother, and they'd talked on the phone, and he'd gone up to visit her a few times, but it'd been hard on a teenage relationship. She had seemed so stressed at his last two visits, and he found himself spending all the time he wasn't visiting Cass with Abby.

It wasn't anything new, the two of them hanging out. It was like every summer of his memory, really.

But there had been moments—maybe he'd imagined it? Maybe it had been wishful thinking?—where he'd thought . . .

He had loved Cass, but Abby . . . Abby knew him in a way no one else really ever did. She'd been the one he used to run to when his dad got a little too drunk. They'd lie together in the meadow between their homes, among the lupine and California poppies, and they'd never talk about the distrust each of their father's choices wore in their hearts, but they *understood* each other. And the older they got, the deeper that understanding went, and the more his teenage self realized that as much as he loved Cass, he didn't have that with her.

And that maybe he wanted that.

Maybe he wanted Abby.

Looking back, when Cass's murder was a

fresh wound in him, he'd pushed it down. The wondering. The attraction. Those thoughts that had bubbled to the surface in the hot summer nights when it was just him and Abby. The want that he could feel in the very tips of his fingers when she shot him that tilted smile.

He'd denied it until he almost believed it had never existed. There had just been one night, right before they both left for college. And there'd been one quick, tear-filled kiss that wasn't about either of them. It was about Cass. It was about goodbye. To the people they'd been. To the bond they had. To the girl whose death had helped define them.

But he'd been able to excuse that simple kiss as grief and it hadn't broken them, because they could still deny it. Deny the want simmering under the surface.

Until Abby's dad died and he'd showed up on her porch after the funeral. He hadn't been able to stop himself from getting on a plane as soon as he was able to. It killed him he hadn't been able to attend the service, but he'd been on a case.

He thought at least he could give her distraction and a bottle of whiskey and his company as she grieved.

But he'd fucked it up. He'd let his guard down and let everything he felt show on his face and then he'd bent forward and . . .

Kissing Abby—*really* kissing her—was just like he thought it would be. And at the same time, nothing like he thought it'd be. It was like the harvest sunset and bright, crisp apples and the comfort of a woman's hand resting over your heart. It was Abby and it was him and it was *right*.

Until she pulled away. And then everything— all those secret dreams he'd been harboring for longer than he'd like to admit—shattered.

He wasn't sure they'd ever get back to normal. Even now, even with this—the hunt—bringing them together. The way she looked at him was wary, like she was worried he might be her downfall.

He pulled onto the road leading to the Winthrop Orchard, driving down the dirt lane, the rows of almond trees blurring as the tires kicked up dust and he veered around the big pothole near the end of the road.

He didn't see Zooey's rental car in the driveway, but Abby's truck was parked under the big oak tree. And she was sitting on the porch in the swing.

"Hey," he said, as he got out of the car and ambled up to the porch. "You are not going to believe what your ex did."

"My . . ." She trailed off, puzzled. "Ryan?"

"He decided to pull a power play and check the evidence box out of the locker before I could. Sheriff Alan's getting an earful from me later."

"Oh," Abby said.

Paul frowned. "What's wrong?" he asked. "How did your talk with the doctor go?"

Abby met his eyes for the first time and his stomach clenched, the worry in them sending a chill through him.

"I need to tell you something," she said. "About Cass."

"What about her?" he asked. "What did Dr. Jeffrey say?"

"Paul," she reached over, taking his hand in hers. "Cass was pregnant."

"What?" He thought he'd misheard her. Surely he had misheard her. "No," he said. "That's . . . no . . ."

"She was," Abby said. "Dr. Jeffrey left it off the report because he thought Mrs. Martin couldn't take it. He buried it."

"No!" Paul repeated. His ears were ringing. The weight was back, pressing on his chest. He could almost feel Mancuso's breath against his cheek as he flashed back to the bomber threatening him, threatening the teen girl he was trying so hard to protect.

"Dr. Jeffrey is wrong," he said firmly. *God, he had to be wrong. Please, let him be wrong.*

"He's not," Abby said. "Paul, I am so sorry. I know this is incredibly hard. It's a whole new loss. But—"

Paul jerked his hand away from her, standing up swiftly. "Abigail," he said sharply, and she startled, her eyes growing wide at his harsh tone. "Cass could not have been pregnant. Not with my baby, at least."

"What are you talking about?"

"Cass and I never had sex," Paul said, and he felt it clawing inside him, the truth that he didn't want to face and now had to. "I wasn't a virgin when we got together, but she was. She wanted to wait until she was at least engaged. I respected that. If she was pregnant . . ."

"The baby wasn't yours," Abby finished.

CHAPTER 21

For the second time that day, Abby felt like she'd been punched. Her mind was going in all sorts of directions, spinning all the possibilities.

Had Cass been raped? She didn't want to voice this question to Paul, even though she knew his thoughts must be going there as well.

Or had Cass cheated on Paul? God, she hoped it was the latter.

Had that been why she was so insecure about his and Abby's friendship? Because she had been unfaithful herself? But with who?

"God, this is a fucking mess," Paul said, and he slumped down in his seat, his eyes sad and hopeless.

"I'm so sorry, Paul," Abby said, trying to tamp down the guilt rising inside her. Once again, she'd tangled them all together. Once again, she was making choices that were hurting the people she loved most.

"She . . . she never gave you any clue that she was pregnant? Or that maybe she'd been assaulted?" Paul asked.

Abby shook her head. She knew, like her, he was frantically tracing back every interaction with Cass during that time period, examining the memories of each conversation with new eyes.

"That doesn't mean an assault isn't what happened," she said. "Every survivor reacts to sexual assault differently. Dr. Jeffrey did say she was at least three months along, so it meant she got pregnant before she left for her grandmother's."

"So there were at least three months where she was . . ." Paul trailed off, his fists clenching. "I hope to God she was cheating on me," he said, his voice hoarse. "I hope she was just being a reckless teenager, and no one hurt her even more. If they did . . ." He raised a shaky hand to his mouth.

Abby went to him, unable to stop herself. Without another word, she crossed the space between them on the porch and slid into his arms, hugging him tight.

"You are a good man," she whispered into

his neck, unable to pull back enough to meet his eyes. His hands were warm, resting high on her hip, and it made her want to shiver, but she steeled herself instead, the denial running too deep for her to fight it. She forced herself to step away, sitting back on the porch swing.

"Cass wasn't perfect," she said. "She might have made some mistakes. But she loved you."

"I know," Paul said. "And I loved her. I will always love the memory of her. But being in love with her? It's a memory too. I'm not hurt if she was cheating on me, Abby. It was a long time ago. We were babies. We had no concept of what *forever* really meant. I'm a completely different person now—and a realist. We would've likely made it to college and then broken up midfreshman year like most couples who try to do it long distance in college do. But this?" His eyes glittered. "A pregnancy changes things. It changes the case. It changes the profile of our unsub."

Abby hadn't even thought of that. She'd been so focused, first, on breaking the news to Paul, that she hadn't even considered how it would affect the case.

"How so?" she asked.

"One of the times a woman is most in danger from an abusive partner is when she's pregnant," Paul said. "I know it's messed up," he said, obviously seeing the horrified look on her face. "But it introduces a motive here that we hadn't considered."

"You're saying you think whoever got Cass pregnant is her killer," Abby said.

"It's very likely," Paul said.

"That means she had to be sexually assaulted," Abby said. "I don't think she would've been with someone much older. And there's no way Dr. X's student was another teenager."

"Not necessarily," said a voice.

Abby, on edge from everything, nearly jumped a foot in the air. Zooey had obviously pulled up the back way and she hadn't heard her come up from the back porch.

"Sorry," Zooey said, taking in her startled breathing. "I just got back from talking to Dr. Jeffrey again. The good news is he did remember some detail . . . but the bad news is I don't think any of it is going to help us pin this guy down." She sat down next to Abby on the porch swing, looking defeated.

"He doesn't have the original pages of the report?" Paul asked.

Abby shook her head. "Apparently Sheriff Baker had them. Who knows where they are? Mrs. Baker sold the house and moved to Florida last year, so I can't even ask her if I can go dig through his old files."

"Shit," Paul said.

"You know what this means," Zooey said, looking meaningfully at Paul.

Abby watched in confusion as the blood drained out of Paul's face. That was *not* a good sign.

"Okay, someone clue the non-FBI crime-solver person in here," she said. "What does this mean?"

Zooey pressed her lips together, her big eyes staring at the porch floorboards like they were the most interesting thing ever.

"Why do both of you look like you want to eat your own tongues?" Abby demanded, a horrible prickle spreading up her spine.

"The next step here is to get more forensic evidence," Paul explained. "That's the only way to move forward at this point, since we don't have any leads."

"Okay," Abby said slowly, still not understanding. "But there isn't a crime scene anymore."

"This isn't about collecting forensic evidence from the crime scene," Paul said. "This is about collecting forensic evidence from Cass."

Abby felt her entire body go to ice and she realized what Paul was saying.

"You . . . you want to *dig her up*?" She was up off

the porch swing, looming over him, her hands balled into fists and her eyes shooting fire. "Are you . . . how . . . oh, my God, *no*. Absolutely not. What would we say to Mrs. Martin? No. There has to be another way."

"Abby—" Zooey started to say.

"*No.*" Abby held her hand out, staring daggers at the younger woman. "No," she said again, and her voice shook and her eyes burned, her throat thick with tears that were about to spill. She turned her attention to Paul, her voice lowering to a deadly serious promise as she said, "You even go near her grave with a shovel and you'll be looking down the barrel of my Winchester and your mama's and every damn woman around here I can round up!"

"Okay, that's enough," Paul said, getting up and grabbing her arm. "We're going to talk in private." But she shook him off angrily.

"No fucking way," she snarled, before stalking into her house, slamming the door shut behind her.

He didn't follow.

He knew better.

SHE GOT UPSTAIRS to her bedroom, where Roscoe was fast asleep on her duvet cover, before sinking down to the ground in tears. Oh,

God, *Cass*. Everything that she'd been tamping down—for *years* now, as she investigated this—started flooding through her body. Her heart began to race, and she wanted so badly to fall apart. She wanted to stay in her room and never come out and just forget about all of this.

But it wasn't who she was. She was her father's stubborn girl. And she would see this through to the very end.

Roscoe whined, having been woken by her tears, and jumped off the bed, meandering over to her and nudging her face with his nose.

"It's okay, boy," she whispered, even though it was so far from okay, she didn't even know how they'd gotten here.

She sniffed, wiping the tears off her cheeks, trying to take in a breath that wasn't shaky.

One of the hardest things she'd ever done was read Cass's autopsy report—what there was of it—and look at the crime scene photos. And she would be damned if she traumatized poor Mrs. Martin by digging her child up and subjecting her to that horror.

There had to be another way.

She had to find a lead. She was the journalist. That was what she was good at.

Still wiping her tears away, Abby got to her feet, feeling shaky but determined. Her purse was tossed on her bed next to her laptop, and she dug inside it, where she'd tucked the piece of paper with Jayden's phone number on it. Maybe Keira Rice's best friend had some information that could be helpful.

Knowing she probably looked like hell, she went into her bathroom and splashed water on her face, and then came back into her bedroom and booted up her laptop. She clicked open her Skype app, logged in, typed Jayden's phone number in, and sent her a friend request. In the "message" box, she wrote: *I want to talk about Keira.*

She could hear Zooey's and Paul's voices—indistinct murmurs—floating through the open window, and she tried to ignore the anger she felt flashing through her.

She knew Zooey was a scientist. She understood that dead bodies and exhuming them was maybe nothing new to either of them in their line of work. But it was *Cass.* Paul should understand.

A pregnancy changes the case, he'd said. Maybe he was right. Maybe the only way to catch Cass's killer was to figure out who the father of her baby was.

But surely there was a different way of doing that than digging her up.

Abby drummed her fingers against the edge

of the computer as her call to Jayden Michaels still went unanswered.

The video call rang and rang, no one picking up. Just when Abby was about to press Cancel, the screen suddenly changed, *Call Accepted* flashing across the computer.

The face of a girl around eighteen or nineteen, her hair pulled in a high ponytail, appeared. She was frowning at the screen, and her oversized tank top and her messy hair made Abby think she might've caught her on her way back from a workout.

"Sorry, I think you have the wrong number," she said.

"Are you Jayden Michaels?" Abby asked.

Jayden frowned. "Yeah."

"I need to talk to you about Keira Rice," Abby said. "I'm working with the FBI on a case."

Jayden's eyes widened. "You . . . did you find Keira?" she asked, her voice shaky on her best friend's name.

"That's one of the things we're trying to do," Abby explained. "We had a meeting with Keira's father and had the chance to look around her room. I noticed that you still call her."

Jayden's cheeks turned a dull red. "What were you doing snooping in Keira's room?" she demanded.

"Jayden, I get it," Abby said gently. "Almost sixteen years ago, my best friend was killed. I know how hard it is to lose your best friend. But the thing is? I think the person who killed my best friend is the same person who took Keira. Which is why I'm here."

"What? You think Keira's like, with a serial killer?" Jayden asked, mouth open. "This isn't an episode of *Criminal Minds*!"

"We've uncovered a pattern," Abby explained. "And Keira's disappearance falls into that pattern. What we're trying to do is figure out everything that happened the night she disappeared. If there was anything unusual. If she talked about meeting someone or being creeped out by someone."

"No," Jayden said, much too quickly. More red crawled up her face. "You want the details, you read the police report. If you're *really* FBI, you can get it."

"Jayden, why do you call Keira every Wednesday?" Abby asked. "I noticed it when I looked at her missed call log. You call every Wednesday without fail. I thought at first that maybe that was the day of the week she went missing, but she went missing on a Saturday night. So why Wednesday?"

Jayden bit her lip. "It's none of your business," she said.

"It is, though," Abby said. "Look, Jayden, I can have the FBI go to a judge and get him to order you to come up here and talk to us." She had no idea if that was true or if it was an empty threat . . . Paul would probably be furious if he knew, but she didn't care. "I don't want to disrupt your schooling. Why don't you just tell me what really happened here? Because you're obviously holding back."

A long silence, where the teen obviously was fighting against her conscience.

"Do it for Keira," Abby urged softly.

"Fine," Jayden snapped, her eyes brimming with tears. "Fine. I call her every Wednesday because that was the day she was supposed to call *me*, so I knew she was safe . . . after."

"After what?" Abby demanded.

"After she ran off with the guy she was seeing," Jayden said.

Abby's heart lurched in her chest. "She left that night to meet him. Her parents, they aren't, like, mean. She loves them and they love her. But they are *really* old-school. She wasn't allowed to date until college. Those were their rules. And she met this guy at one of our soccer meets I guess and they hit it off. The thing was, he was older."

Abby frowned. "How much older?"

"I don't know," Jayden said. "I never saw them. She never even told me his name. Everything with them was super secret."

"Why didn't you tell anyone this when the police got involved?" Abby asked, trying not to feel frustrated since Jayden had been a sixteen-year-old girl at the time. You did stupid things as a teenager in the name of friendship.

"I really thought she would call," Jayden said. "And then I thought . . . okay, maybe they just went off to Vegas and got married and lived happily ever after?"

But the look on the girl's face told Abby she knew that wasn't what happened. There were tears in her eyes, guilt in every smooth line of her face.

"She's dead, isn't she?" Jayden whispered.

Abby bit her lip. "I don't know," she said. "But I'm trying to find out. Is there *anything* else you knew about this guy? His name? If he was older, did he have a job?"

"I think he had dark hair, because she once compared him to Patrick Dempsey," Jayden said. "She loves *Grey's Anatomy*. She was always talking about the drives they took." Her eyes widened. "His car!" she said, suddenly, excitedly.

"What about his car?" Abby asked.

"There was one time where my parents were out of town, and Keira was spending the night with some of our other friends. Just a big slumber party thing for the girls. But she ended up ditching us, saying she had somewhere to be. I went outside to make sure she got off safe, and I saw his car. It was one of those Karmann Ghias. I remember because my brother loves them. And because it was like, *bright* yellow."

Abby's mouth went dry at her words. "Are you sure?" Abby asked.

"Yeah," Jayden said. "One hundred percent."

"Okay," Abby said, an odd sort of numbness beginning to sweep over her body. "Jayden, thank you. I've got to go."

She barely heard the girl's goodbye as she shut her computer down.

For a moment that seemed frozen, she sat there on her bed, a shaky, horrible sensation of *knowing* sweeping over her as her mind clicked the puzzle pieces together.

She had thought it odd that Sheriff Baker had been the one to discourage the truth in the ME report. Baker had been a good man and a good cop. Cass's murder had been the case that had seemed to finally break him. He'd retired shortly after it.

Had it affected him so because he'd buried evidence? Because he'd chosen to cave to someone with more power instead of doing the right thing?

The only person who had that much power in Castella Rock was the mayor. And back then, the mayor was Dominic Clay.

Her ex-boyfriend Ryan's father.

A hysterical little sound burst from her throat.

She had figured it out.

She knew what happened now.

CHAPTER 22

"Paul! Zooey!"

Paul's head whipped around to the front door at the sound of Abby's shouting. She burst out the door, and instead of being full of fire and anger like he expected, there was wide-eyed realization painted all over her face.

"It's Ryan Clay," she said. "Cass's killer is Ryan Clay."

"What?" He stared at her, trying to make sense.

"The guy who checked out the evidence box?" Zooey asked, clearly confused.

"I just got off the phone with Jayden Michaels," Abby explained. "That's Keira Rice's best friend. It turns out Keira was planning on running off with some guy she was seeing. Jayden didn't know who it was, but she told me that he drove a yellow Karmann Ghia."

Paul's eyes widened. He remembered when

Ryan's father had gifted him the vintage car in high school. He used to park it sideways in the student parking lot, like an asshole. "Are you sure?" he asked.

"Yes," Abby said.

"Okay, but it's just a car," Zooey said. "There must be other people around here with the same one."

"That's not a common car around here," Abby said. "Especially that color. And Ryan's had the car since high school. Think about it, Paul," she said. "Sheriff Baker, who by all accounts was honest as hell, decides to mess with evidence in the biggest homicide investigation this town has ever seen. Why would he do that unless he had some major external pressure?"

"From Mayor Clay, you're thinking?" Paul asked.

"Yes." Abby nodded eagerly. "And why would the mayor do that?"

"To protect Ryan," Paul answered. "If it got out that Cass was pregnant, then everyone would've thought I was the father. They would've done a DNA test to confirm and when it didn't . . ."

"They'd start digging into who else might've been with Cass—or assaulted her," Abby finished. "Ryan must have gone to his father and gotten him to cover it up."

"Ryan was the father of Cass's baby," Paul said. "That's the easiest explanation here. Her pregnancy could've been the stressor that caused him to snap and kill her. He didn't need to tell his dad that to get him to cover it up, all he had to do was say that the baby might be his. That would've been enough for a cover-up, because it would've made him a suspect."

"There's something in that evidence box," Abby said with surety. "That's why he took it. Not to mess with you or to be an ass. As soon as he found out you were looking into Cass's case, he knew it was just a matter of time until you made the connection."

"I need to call Sheriff Alan," Paul said grimly. "We've got to find the connections between Clay and the rest of the missing girls."

"Okay, wait a minute," Zooey declared. "I agree that Clay is a good lead that we need to pursue. But we're not factoring in one big thing here: Dr. X. Do we really think Ryan is X's apprentice?"

"Wouldn't that play into the idea of the leader/follower relationship you told me most killing pairs fall into?" Abby asked Paul.

"He would've had to get him really young," Paul said. "He would've needed . . . practice." He winced at the look on Abby's face. Sometimes it was hard to remember a time when all this information about death, murder, and killers wasn't in his head. But when he saw how she reacted sometimes, it all came rushing back; how desensitized he was to the horrors of the world. "What do you think, Zooey?"

"From what Grace has taught me about adolescent killers, he would've shown signs when you all were kids. You had a relationship with him, Abby. Was he violent? Controlling?"

"He wasn't violent to me, but he was bossy. And he got into a lot of fights."

"I had to pull him off a boy he was trying to beat to death with his cleats when we were in baseball," Paul said grimly. "I don't doubt he's capable of killing someone."

"He was also working on Cass, behind my back," Abby said.

Paul frowned. "What are you talking about?"

"When Ryan broke up with me when we were seventeen, he said it was because you and I were too close," Abby said, her cheeks pinkening. "And then he went to Cass and said the same thing. He got in her head because she confronted me about it. That's the reason I didn't go visit her at her grandma's that year like I usually did."

Paul's stomach clenched. She was just telling him this now? Why had she held this back for so many years? This revelation suddenly made some of Cass's behavior that summer make sense. She had been always asking about Abby and what she was doing when she was gone that month. And there had been a wariness in her voice whenever Paul had, in his teenage boy obliviousness, cheerfully recounted his days spent with Abby.

Had Ryan got in Cass's head, making her think he and Abby had a thing on the side going on, and Cass turned to him only to find herself pregnant? Had that been part of this sick game of his, to set up Cass and then cut her down, literally and figuratively?

Jesus. His gut lurched, sickness rising in his chest. He needed to find this bastard. And make him pay.

"I'm tracking him down," Paul declared. "He has some shit to answer for, no matter what."

He pulled his cell phone out of his pocket, dialing Sheriff Alan's number. It clicked to voice mail. Alan was probably out hunting the arsonist still. On a hunch, he dialed dispatch. And sure enough, it was Ted Phillips, an old friend of his dad's, who picked up.

"Castella County Sheriff's Dispatch, how may I direct your call?"

"Hi, Ted, it's Paul Harrison," he said.

"Paul! I heard you were in town."

"Listen, Ted, I'm trying to track down Deputy Clay. You happen to know where he is?"

"Let me check the logs," Ted said. There was a tapping noise. "Huh. Looks like Ryan had a shift today, but he didn't show up. Or call in sick."

Of course he didn't. Fuck. He was already on the run. He'd had an entire day's head start.

"Thanks, Ted." Paul hung up. "He didn't show up for work," he said.

"What do we do?" Abby asked. "How do we find him?"

"He may be in the wind. Or he may go to ground," Paul said. "Hide out somewhere."

"If he's keeping the missing girls for a two-year cycle, that means he needs a remote area. Somewhere he can keep them captive and alive and unnoticed," Zooey said.

"You think he *keeps them*?" Abby asked, like the idea hadn't even occurred to her.

Zooey bit her lip, shooting an uncertain look at Paul, who gave her the barest of nods.

"The two-year cycle between girls seems to suggest that yes, he keeps them alive for a certain amount of time," Zooey said. "And when he's . . . used them up, he disposes of them. And replaces them with a new girl."

"This is sick," Abby said, looking white as a sheet. "I *dated* him. Oh, my *God*."

"It's okay," Paul said, reaching out, squeezing her shoulder softly, even though it was so far from not. He understood the fear and horror on her face. He was feeling it too.

Had Ryan raped Cass? Or had they had consensual sex? If it had been consensual, had it been the pregnancy that had triggered his rage? Paul knew Cass, she would've kept the baby. Had that been the thing that pushed Ryan over the edge?

Or had he been planning to kill her the whole time? Had seeding doubt in her mind about her boyfriend and her best friend been the first in a series of steps that were always going to lead to Cass dead under the olive trees? Was this all just a way for Ryan to show off for the man who had shaped him into a killer?

There were so many possibilities here. Too many possibilities. Until he was across an interrogation table from the bastard, he wasn't going to get any answers.

They needed to find him. And fast.

"Where would he be?" Paul thought out loud.

"What about the Clays' hunting cabin?" Abby

asked. "It butts up right against the national forest. He took me up there a few times. There's no one for miles."

Of course. The Clays had had their hunting cabin in the Siskiyou Mountains for decades. The mayor had been a big trophy hunter back in the day.

"That sounds like a serial killer's wet dream," Zooey said. "What do you think, boss? Do we call in the cavalry?"

"I have an idea," Paul said. "But it's risky."

"I eat risky for breakfast," Abby said. "Tell me."

For a second, all he could see was her. For a moment, all he could think was *you're mine* and *I think I love you* and *this is the biggest mess I've ever been in and I'm so damn grateful I'm there with you.*

He took a deep breath. And then he told her.

CHAPTER 23

"Who is this guy we're going to see again?" Abby asked, as Paul navigated her truck up the narrow dirt road, the thick pine forest looming on either side. Zooey was squished between them, her computer open on her lap. Abby had no idea how she wasn't carsick.

"Cyrus Rooke," Paul said. "He's a search and rescue specialist. And guide."

"What kind of guide?" Abby asked as they climbed farther up the mountain. He'd driven them out to the middle of nowhere and she was starting to get skeptical over this plan of his.

"Wilderness. Mountain. Desert. Jungle. You name a terrain, he can bring you through it. I met him when he was working for the military, but he retired a few years ago. Gave me a call when he settled in the Siskiyous. Told me to look him up if I ever got home again."

"You think he can find Ryan?" Abby asked.

Paul shrugged. "That's not really what we're here for," he said mysteriously, coming to a stop in front of a giant wooden gate. There were spikes—wooden ones, carved out of what looked like tree trunks—rising from the top of the gate and a sign that said: *Trespassers will be shot.*

"Oh, this is going to be pleasant," Zooey declared, as Paul honked his horn, three short bursts.

After a long moment when the camera affixed to one of the fence beams just blinked at them, with a scraping sound, the gate swung open to reveal a man.

He was pretty much what you'd expect a search and rescue specialist and all-terrain expert to be. Massive and well-muscled, he wore a flannel shirt and faded jeans. His curly black hair was pulled back at the base of his neck, a few strands left to dip into his dark, penetrating eyes. He pointed down the road, and Paul drove down it. Abby turned around in her seat, watching the man follow them.

They stopped at a log cabin, one he'd likely built himself—set in the little clearing carved out of the thick forest. There was smoke chugging out of the river rock chimney, and Abby could see a chicken coop and a garden beyond it.

Abby got out of the truck, and Zooey scooted across the bench seat to follow her. Paul strode up to Cyrus Rooke, holding out his hand.

But Cyrus, a veritable bear of a man, swept him up in a hug, clapping him hard on the back. "Harrison!" he boomed, his voice so deep it was almost a growl. "How are you, old dog?"

Old dog? Zooey mouthed at Abby, who shot her an equally puzzled look.

"Cy, it's great to see you." Paul grinned.

"We'll catch up later," Cyrus said. He looked over to Abby and Zooey, nodding at them. "Ma'am. Ma'am."

"This is Abby. She brought the case to me. And this is Zooey. She works with me in DC. She's head of my forensics team."

"Nice to meet both of you," Cyrus said. "Come inside. We'll get to work."

Cyrus's cabin may have looked rustic on the outside, but the inside was another story. Half of the living room was filled with a computer setup that made Zooey look like cartoon hearts were about to pop out of her eyes.

"I've pulled up the sat feed on the coordinates you gave me," Cy said to Paul, leading the three of them over to the computer monitor, where a fuzzy black-and-white image of what looked like a cabin's roof in the middle of the woods was on the screen. "There's been movement in the last two hours."

"So he's there," Paul said.

"Most likely," Cy said.

"How did you even get access to these feeds?" Zooey asked.

"I've got my ways," Cy said with a wink. "So, if we zoom out—" he clicked a few things, and the image changed, giving them a better view of the forest "—we can see there's a back road right here." He drew his finger along the narrow line of gray snaking through the trees behind the Clays' hunting cabin. "This is where I'll park. Zooey will stay in the truck with the radio. Harrison, you'll come down from the north, I'll come up from the south, and Abby? You know how to use a gun?"

Abby nodded. She was starting to realize Paul's friend, the "wilderness guide," was more of an off-grid badass—the guy you send in during a hostage crisis.

"You come in from the east. Then, Harrison, it's your show."

Paul nodded. "Let's see . . . Abby, you'll be coming right up where his truck is," he explained, pointing to the east area on the screen. "So take it out. Really simple, just slash the tires so he can't escape that way. Cy? You and I flank

the cabin and throw flash-bangs through each
of the windows. They go off, we go in, subdue,
and cuff him. Then we'll call the sheriff so we
can bring him down to the station for interrogation."

"Classic," Cyrus said. "We just gotta make
sure he doesn't bolt for the woods through the
west side."

"He does that, he'll come right up against me."
Zooey pointed to the spot where Cyrus had in-
dicated the truck would be parked.

Cyrus looked at her, cocking an eyebrow.
"You a good shot?"

"No, she isn't," Paul said, looking like there
was a story behind that as Zooey pursed her
lips.

"I've taken a lot of classes with Agent Walker
since then!" she protested.

"You almost shot yourself in the foot," he said.
"Absolutely not. You get a beanbag gun."

"You can't hold that one little mistake against
me forever." Zooey pouted, while Abby tried
to hide her smile. Their dynamic, it turned out,
was very much like disapproving but loving father and precocious child, which Abby guessed
made sense, considering Paul had been the one
to usher Zooey out of a life of crime and into
the FBI.

"I can hold any action I want against you when your well-being's at risk," he said. "I'm the team leader. If you shoot yourself with the beanbag gun, at least you're not gonna blow off a foot or a hand. You'll just break it. And then I'll have less paperwork to file."

"Like you do your own paperwork," Zooey sneered. "You totally bribe Rhonda with those butter cookies so she'll do it for you."

"Wow, it's like watching a dad and his teenager," Cyrus remarked to Abby, who had to laugh at their synchronicity. "Just, you know, FBI-style."

"They're a trip," she agreed. She looked up at him, her smile warming. "I really appreciate you doing this," she said as Paul and Zooey continued to argue.

"Harrison's a good guy," Cyrus said. "I kinda owe him. He got me out of a tough spot a few years back."

Of course he had. For someone who loved the rules so much, Paul apparently had a lot of friends who seemed to skate past them with ease. There was no way the sat feeds Cyrus was accessing were a legal tap.

"Fine," Zooey huffed. "I'll take the damn beanbag gun."

"Glad to hear it," Paul said. "Cy, you got vests for us?"

Cyrus nodded. "Stuff's in the back shed. Come on, we'll go get it. Ladies, there's a trunk in the back room there that's full of clothes suited for an op like this."

"Find whatever's comfortable, not too loose, and make sure it's dark," Paul directed. "Change into it. We'll be hitting the hunting cabin as soon as the sun sets."

The two men left the cabin, and for a second, Abby and Zooey just looked at each other.

"You nervous?' Abby asked, as they walked over to the back room and the chest in question.

"We're in good hands," Zooey said. "I'd like more backup, but we're kind of doing this under the radar." She plucked a black shirt out of the trunk, tossing it to Abby, who found a pair of dark cargo pants that looked like they'd fit her. "I'm gonna go try these," she said.

Her stomach was jumping by the time she'd changed into the clothes. It took a few deep breaths over the sink to gather herself.

She was a farm girl, so she'd grown up with a rifle in her hand, to ward off predators and to hunt with her father. It was one of the few activities that seemed to cheer him, so they'd spent a lot of time in the woods when she was younger.

But hunting deer and hunting a man were two very different things. When she walked back into the cabin's main room and found Paul and Cyrus loading weapons and flash-bombs into a duffel, her stomach clenched.

God, she was a journalist, not an FBI agent. She had no training to do this.

But there wasn't much choice. She was in this to the very end. Just like Paul.

"You know how to use this?" Cyrus asked, handing her a bolt-action shotgun.

She took it, the weight of it almost a comfort in her hands, and nodded.

"You willing to use it?" he asked, and there was something searching in his eyes that made her go cold, that made her want to shrivel away from him and hide. This was a guy who had seen some *shit* go down—maybe even been the cause of it. And if she didn't fall into line and have his back, she'd be in trouble.

"I am," she said.

"Good."

He moved away, and Paul came up to her, handing her a black beanie.

"Your friend is very intense," she said, pulling

the hat on, trying to hide the beacon that was her red hair.

"Here, let me," he said, and he reached over, twisting her hair and then tucking it gently into the hat. She tried not to suck in a sharp breath when his fingers brushed against the nape of her neck, but she couldn't stop herself.

His eyes flickered, dropping down to her mouth, and she thought about how this could be it. She could get shot and die out in the woods tonight. And she would've never told him . . .

The regrets threatened to swamp her, because this wasn't the right time and it wasn't the right place and she had never, ever felt like the right girl.

"Thanks," she whispered, because she was a coward.

He smiled. "Any time."

"Harrison, how many flash-bangs do you want to bring?" Cyrus called, and Paul turned away, the moment breaking.

Abby tugged the hat down over her ears and hurried over to Zooey, to check on the restraints.

The sun was setting soon.

And then the hunt for Ryan would be on.

CHAPTER 24

Paul traveled, low and quiet, through the forest. Darkness had fallen, and as he moved through the underbrush, he couldn't help but think of the last time he was doing the same thing, creeping toward a cabin that held a dangerous man.

The Mancuso case had been a turning point for him, even though he hadn't realized it at the time. He'd been too reckless then. Unable to listen to Maggie's instincts, too intent on being the one who was right.

He was leaving that behind and focusing on the future . . . as soon as he was finally able to put his past to rest.

Ryan held the answers to questions he hadn't even realized he was supposed to have. And Paul was going to hear all of them.

"I'm in position," Zooey said over the radio

from her spot on the old mining road, half a mile north.

"Approaching the tree line," Cyrus said. "Abby, are you in position?"

"Just a second," she said, sounding a little out of breath. "Nearly to the truck."

"Remember, a quick stab of the knife," Paul said. "Then drag down. You'll need to put some muscle into it."

"Got it," she said.

He'd reached the tree line and flattened himself against a trunk, squinting in the weak light of the moon, trying to spot Abby.

There she was, a dark blur coming from the east, circling around the truck that was parked in front of the cabin. He watched, counting silently as she hit the first tire, then the second, then the final two.

"Tires are done."

"Fall back," Paul ordered. "Find a place in the tree line. Stay hidden. And keep your eyes on the front door."

He waited a beat and then said, "Let me know when you're out of sight."

Another tense minute passed, and then: "I'm out of the way."

"Zooey, stay sharp. Cy, start the count," Paul ordered.

Cy began to count from ten, and the two men moved in unison, coming at the cabin from two sides. They moved like a well-oiled machine, the flash-bangs they tossed through the windows going off, four deafening bangs, one right after another, echoing through the forest, as light brightened the clearing like lightning.

Paul had circled back to the front door, and as soon as the light cleared, he kicked open the front door, his gun drawn, Cy at his back as they charged inside. "Hands in the air!"

Paul peered through the smoke of the flash-bangs rising in the air and as it cleared, he saw what was slumped over in the chair set in the middle of the rustic cabin.

"Christ," Cy swore, taking in the sight as they both lowered their guns.

Ryan Clay was dead, half of his skull missing, blown away, presumably, with the double-barrel shotgun that was lying on the ground next to him.

"What's going on?" Zooey asked over the radio.

"Zooey, I need you to get down here," Paul said. "We've got a dead body you need to look at."

"Ryan Clay?" she asked.

"Yup," Paul said.

"He's dead?" Abby asked over her own radio. "I'm on my way."

Paul, thinking about how Abby reacted to the mere possibility of exhuming Cass's body, cursed, shutting his radio off. "I'm gonna head Abby off," he told Cy. "This is . . ." He made a face, staring down at Ryan's body.

Headshots were always messy.

"She doesn't need to see this," he finished. "She's a civilian."

"I understand," Cy said. "Go protect your woman."

Paul couldn't deny the satisfaction of Abby being cast as his. It was a base kind of desire that he probably should be more enlightened about, but right now, he felt on edge, primed to protect.

Things weren't right here. He'd wait for Zooey's expert opinion, but all his knowledge and training was telling him that Ryan didn't kill himself.

He stepped down off the porch as Abby approached through the darkness, the rifle strap slung across her chest. She looked like the kind of woman who went off to fight wars, tall and strong and willing to do anything, no matter the cost.

"It's bad," he said.

"I figured," she said, crossing her arms. She looked over his shoulder, at the cabin door and swallowed audibly, her throat working frantically like she was building up the courage to go inside.

His heart squeezed at the little movement. She was so strong. So damn determined to be there, every step of the way.

I owe Cass, she had said, that first day, when she was trying to convince him of all of this. God, had that just been five days ago? It felt like an eternity. Part of him, when he was with Abby, felt like he'd never left home. And another part of him was *only* aware of how long it'd been. How much they'd both changed.

But deep down, their cores, their hearts, they were still the same. Which is why it was so hard to shake the want, the need to comfort her, to protect her, to keep her with him, close to him, safe with him.

"You don't want to go in there," he said.

She glared at him, her eyes growing heated. "Why do you always try to protect me from *everything*?" she demanded.

Because you're reckless, he thought. *Because you make me want to be reckless. Because the idea of someone hurting you anymore makes me want to use whatever power I have to crush them to dust.*

"Because someone needs to," he said, and her chin tilted up stubbornly.

"I'm a big girl, Harrison," she said. "I've seen plenty of crime scene photos."

"Abby, trust me here," he said softly. "You don't want to see this. Do you really want to see the boy who you used to kiss and hold hands with with half of his head missing?"

She sucked in a sharp breath, her green eyes widening, a dark flush rising on her freckled cheeks. She opened her mouth to say something, but was interrupted by the sound of an engine rumbling toward them. Zooey came driving down the road in the truck and hopped out. She reached into the back, pulled out her messenger bag, and headed to the porch. Paul and Abby watched as she suited up, pulling booties over her shoes and tucking her hair back.

"Cyrus," she called. "I'm gonna need you to get out of there. I don't want any more contamination of my crime scene."

"You're pretty bossy for a nerd," the mountain man commented as he ambled out of the cabin.

"Haven't you heard? All nerds are bossy," Zooey drawled sarcastically. "All of you, stay out here," she directed. "I want to get a feel for the scene without all your reactions clogging up the science."

Without another word, she disappeared into the cabin. The three of them stood on the porch, falling into an awkward silence as the adrenaline from the initial ambush began to fade.

Paul's mind was working through it, what this meant. He kept his hand on the gun at his hip, aware that if someone had killed Ryan, he very well might be out there, somewhere, watching . . . waiting.

Who the hell were they dealing with here?

The cabin door opened and Zooey stepped out, a somber expression on her face. In her hand, was a small leather-bound bible, which she gave to Paul after he pulled on the pair of gloves she handed him.

"Last page," she said.

Paul thumbed to the back of the bible, his heart thumping when he realized what he was reading.

This was the Clay family bible, an old one, where the births and deaths of each member of the family were recorded. And at the very bottom, there was an addition that made his stomach drop:

Baby 2002–2002 Lost with her mother

He took a deep breath, steeling himself and looked to Zooey. "What do we know?" he asked.

"Okay, first of all, there's no way that guy shot himself," Zooey said. "The blood splatter's all wrong. Hell, even the shotgun on the floor's at the wrong angle. Plus, there is bruising on his wrists that indicates he was tied. Few tests, and I bet I'll find rope fibers in his skin."

"So it's a staged suicide," Paul said.

"Not a very good one," Cy muttered.

"He's right," Zooey said. "This is pretty damn messy."

Abby frowned. "That doesn't make sense. If Ryan was killed by Dr. X's apprentice . . . our unsub is good enough to frame an infamous serial killer. But he can't stage a suicide?"

"You're also right," Zooey said. "Which is why I say we get the hell out of here. Now. Because he's probably out there, lurking in the woods, waiting to pick us off, like a creepy, murderous lumberjack."

Abby looked over her shoulder nervously.

"Your geek's right, Paul," Cy said, shooting a sly glance at the annoyed way Zooey pursed her lips. "This is starting to feel like a setup."

Paul peered at the tree line. Part of him wanted to shout into the darkness: *Come and get me*. But he couldn't. He might have, if it had just been

Cy and him. Cy was the kind of man who you wanted at your back with this sort of thing. But he wasn't putting Abby or Zooey in that kind of danger.

Zooey had signed on for that when she joined the FBI. But Abby hadn't.

"Let's go," Paul said, his mind made up. "Get in the truck with Cy," he said. "I'm going to do one final search of the cabin."

He waited until he was sure they were secure in the truck with Cy before going back inside.

The evidence box Ryan had taken was sitting on the kitchen table, and Paul went over and grabbed it. For a moment, he just stood in the middle of the cabin, acutely aware of the body out of the corner of his eye.

Ryan Clay had been a narcissistic, misogynistic asshole who loved power plays and apparently also loved taking advantage of teenage girls' naiveté, if his "relationship" with Keira Rice was any indication, and he was likely the father of Cass's baby, but he hadn't killed Cass.

No, he'd been the unsub's patsy. A failsafe that had been planned *years* in advance, just in case someone ever got far enough to connect Keira Rice's disappearance with Cass's murder.

But why stage the scene so badly? That was the question. Paul puzzled over it as he carried the box back to the truck, setting it in the bed before climbing inside.

As they drove away, Paul kept an eye on his phone, and as soon as they were back in cell phone range, he called Sheriff Alan and told him he'd need to send the deputies out.

There was a crime scene to take care of.

CHAPTER 25

Abby felt like she'd been through a war where no one was the victor. By the time Zooey had headed off to her motel, and Cyrus had disappeared, practically fading into the mist like some sort of cowboy of yore, it was late.

Roscoe was snoozing upstairs, drooling on her pillow like it was his own, so she went downstairs. She checked the corkboard in the mudroom, seeing that Jonah, her orchard manager, had left her a note that said: *Fed Roscoe for you.*

She needed to track Jonah down tomorrow and thank him. She hadn't been checking in at all since Paul had arrived, and that wouldn't do. Jonah had the orchard running like a well-oiled machine, but she liked to be in the know. She didn't want him to feel like the burden of the place was all on him while she reaped the profit. One of the big changes she had made after her father died was to give each of her workers a share in the orchard. This land may have been in her family for generations, but she wasn't going to be the removed owner in the farmhouse, watching like a queen over the serfs who worked her land. All her employees had a hand in the orchard's success—and they deserved a piece of it. It was only fair, when there were entire families who'd worked for her father for decades.

Paul had left for his house, going back across the meadow, and as tired as she was, Abby felt restless and unable to sleep . . . like she'd drunk too much coffee and the jitters were just starting to set in.

She'd been wrong about Ryan. That was clear now. She would feel a flash of guilt for thinking he was a murderer, but apparently, the man preyed on Keira Rice, got into a predatory, illegal relationship with her, and then had never come clean when she disappeared. So she was saving all her sympathy for Keira—and the other girls missing along I-5.

What had happened to Keira? Abby racked her brain, trying to think of the most likely scenario. Their unsub had a type. That meant he sought the girls he took out. Probably stalked them for a while. And Keira had been taken later in the year than the other girls. Had it been harder to get to her? Taking her from a motel parking lot was risky. It was the first time she'd gone to a soccer meet without her parents. Had the unsub just been waiting for his chance to take her, and when she snuck out to meet Ryan, he took advantage of the opportunity presented?

That seemed the most reasonable explanation. If Ryan had showed up late—or Keira had snuck out early—then Ryan could have missed Keira's abduction completely. She could've been gone before he even pulled into the motel parking lot.

Maybe she wasn't cut out for this, she thought miserably.

Even though Paul had held her back from seeing the actual grisly scene, she couldn't help but imagine it, her damn imagination dreaming up scenarios from his warnings. She still felt sick that she'd ever let someone who preyed on teen girls touch her—even though she'd been a teenager herself at the time—and questions about Ryan and Cass still whirled in her head. Paul had shown her the Clay family bible, where Ryan had memorialized his and Cass's baby. It made her stomach hurt, thinking of Cass so alone and so scared as she died in that orchard.

Unable to stop the disturbing thoughts, Abby found herself grabbing a flashlight and heading out into the night, to walk the rows of trees, hoping that if she tired herself out, she could get some sleep.

As she reached the end of the fifth row, she saw movement across the meadow. For a moment, she almost ran, residual fear from what had happened earlier rushing through her body.

But then the clouds over the moon shifted, and she saw it was Paul.

A new kind of tension filled her as she stood there, at the border of the meadow and the orchard, on the edge of . . . *something*.

"Couldn't sleep?" she asked when he was just a foot away from her. His flannel shirt was buttoned crookedly, like he'd done it in the dark, or too fast. It made her want to smile. Such a small, charming, clumsy little thing. It made her want to reach out, to slip the buttons free, and push the shirt off his shoulders.

He shook his head.

"Abby," he said.

Just her name. But it made her heart flutter. It made her want to sway into him. To take comfort in him.

To love him the way he deserved.

"We can't keep doing this," he said. "I . . ." He reached out, and his palm was cupping her cheek and his eyes were on hers, lit with a fire she'd seen before, that she'd run from before.

This time, she wasn't running.

"I'm done," he declared fiercely. "I am done feeling guilty. And I'm done denying things. I've followed the rules," he said, and she felt caught in his gaze, like a moth lured to a light, unable to look or move away. "It's who I am. But you . . ." He stroked the back of his fingers down her cheekbone. Her eyes fluttered closed at the touch, and when they opened, his own were raw with honesty. "You make me want to break all the rules," he whispered.

He kissed her then. It wasn't the first kiss or their second or even their third. It wasn't the kiss of clumsy six-year-olds, bashful and laughing. It wasn't the kiss of hurt teenagers, unable to deal with their grief any way but together. And it wasn't the kiss of adults, angry and lashing out and finally, finally getting what they both wanted, even though it was the wrong time and the wrong place and the wrong way.

He kissed her like he knew her, because he did. He kissed her like it was the start of something new, because it was.

He kissed her because it had been long enough, denying what they both wanted, what they needed:

Each other.

CHAPTER 26

Kissing Abby—really, truly, kissing her, like he'd wanted to do for so long—was like discovering the two of them all over again. The boy he was. The girl she had been. The man he'd become. The woman she was now.

She was all curves and freckles in the moonlight, leading him through rows of trees like a siren. He wanted to chase her, to pound up the stairs of that old farmhouse and make that rickety old bed squeak until the morning hours.

But they didn't even get upstairs. They barely got up off the porch before he was kissing her again, unable to resist, unable to go any longer without touching her, without having her wrapped in his arms.

He wanted to trace every freckle on her skin, to press his lips to each sweet mark. And when he licked over the spattering of dots along her collarbone, she gasped, her fingers twisting in his hair, pulling just slightly, sending a shock of heat right to his cock.

He'd never wanted anyone like this. It was roaring to life in him—denied for so damn long—that it had complete control of him as she whipped his shirt off over his head. He felt out of control and utterly focused at the same time as he pressed her against the wall, greedy, consuming kisses filling the long moments between their gasping breaths.

His hands slid underneath her simple gray t-shirt, the soft skin of her stomach and rib cage—and the sound she made—a Goddamn revelation as he slipped her shirt off. Her skin was like milk sprinkled with specks of saffron and his mouth skated down the lush curves of her breasts, down her stomach, and then he was on his knees and his hands were on the button of her jeans and he was looking up at her, a question in his eyes.

He'd spent so long denying this that now that he wasn't ignoring it or her or this—this intense, alive energy between them that had always been there—he didn't know where he wanted to start. He wanted to rise to his feet and kiss her again. He wanted to stay on his knees and worship her.

He wanted to do everything and anything she ever wanted or dreamed.

She stepped out of her jeans, and then she was standing there, pressed up against the wall of her hallway, dark blue lace and smooth skin and all his. He couldn't quite believe it.

She was the most beautiful woman he'd ever seen, staring at him, just a hint of challenge in her face, and when he made no move toward her she made a little impatient noise.

Her palms, searing hot, cupped his face and she pulled him to her, kissing him. Her teeth nipped along his bottom lip like a dare, her tongue darted out to soothe the spot like an apology. His fingers tightened around her hips as she hitched herself up against him, her thighs—those strong, glorious, freckled thighs of hers—wrapped around his hips.

"Fuck, Abby," he groaned. He could feel the heat of her against the ridge of his cock, pressing painfully against the fly of his jeans. He kissed her, sweeping her hair off her neck and dragging kisses up it as she unbuckled his belt.

Keeping his hand on the delicious curve of her ass, he kicked his pants away and staggered over to the couch, tilting backward onto it. She let out a laughing little shriek, falling on top of him, her legs falling to each side of his hips and with a wicked smile, she moved her hips against him in an agonizingly slow circle.

He choked out her name, the friction making his eyes roll as she reached back and unhooked her bra.

He was the luckiest fucking man alive, he thought, as he cupped one of her breasts, tilting up to kiss her.

She made a little teasing, tutting sound, and then she was lifting off him. The loss of the heat of her body, the lushness of her weight against him, was enough to make him clench his fists. But then she tugged down those blue panties she was wearing and he was clenching his fists for another reason.

"You're gonna be the death of me," he groaned, rearing up and grabbing her, tumbling her into his lap, gloriously, beautifully naked and *his*.

Mine, he thought, as her fingers wrapped around his cock, guiding it to the core of her. She was so slick, so wet, so fucking hot as he slid into her. He was almost overcome by it, the heat, the way her muscles flexed around him and her head tilted back, like she was savoring how full she felt.

He thrust into her, his hands going to her hips. He could feel her getting wetter around him as she ground down on his cock in quick little bursts, her lip caught between her teeth, her eyes fluttering closed as the pleasure—the sensation—built.

He wanted her to come. Wanted to see how her cheeks flushed, how she moaned, how she would tighten around him. He wanted every moan and shudder as she writhed on his cock, lost in the feeling.

"God, you're beautiful," he gritted out, rearing up to kiss her, his hand dropping between their bodies, his knuckles brushing just barely over her clit.

Her nails dug into his shoulders and she shattered, rippling around him. The sight of it, so erotic, so beautiful, so *her*, was all it took. Two more thrusts into her pulsing heat and he was coming, his forehead dropping to her shoulder, his arms tightening around her as pleasure like he'd never known rushed through him.

For a long time, after, they remained clinging to each other, panting, the aftershocks and intimacy almost too much.

Paul didn't know what to say. He didn't know what she wanted to hear. So he just stayed silent, stroking her hair, savoring the feel of her in his arms.

He knew how he felt. He'd known for two

years now. Ever since that night he'd kissed her and then ran.

The time to talk would come later.

He'd been a coward with her, before.

He wouldn't be again.

CHAPTER 27

S he woke with Paul wrapped around her, his long nose pressed into the curve of her neck, his arm looped around her possessively, drawing her close. She snuggled into him, stretched out her body, feeling like she was finally aware of each and every part of her.

For a moment, she was so distracted by this, by the marvel of him in her bed, with him in her arms, that she didn't realize that something had woken her.

His phone was vibrating on the bedside table.

"Paul," she whispered, nudging him.

He murmured, his hold tightening on her. "'Nother five minutes," he muttered.

"Paul." She poked him again. "Your phone."

"Hmm?" He jerked up, squinting at the flash of light from the incoming call. He grabbed it, sitting up in bed. "Georgia?" he said into the phone. "It's two in the morning. What in the—"

His entire body tensed up next to Abby. Her head whipped toward him, the air in the room suddenly changing, as he said, "How long has she been gone?"

Gone? Who was gone? Abby sat up, staring at him urgently. His expression was frozen, his throat working fiercely. "Georgia, I'm on my way. I don't care what the sheriff says about needing it to be twenty-four hours. Tell him he issues the alert or I'll have the FBI director call him personally. Okay? I'll be there in twenty minutes. Stay calm." He hung up, looking at Abby.

"Who?" Abby asked.

"Robin," Paul said, and his voice cracked on his niece's name. "Fuck. He took Robin."

"Oh, my God." Abby leapt out of bed, grabbing her shirt and tossing Paul his own. "We need to go. Are we sure it's him? Maybe she's at a girl-friend's house? Maybe her car broke down?"

"She was supposed to come straight home from her wrestling meet," Paul said. "She didn't come back. She wouldn't run away. Her phone's turned off so we can't track it. She's his type—she has long, curly dark hair and a sweet face. And she's my niece."

Abby yanked her jeans on as he did the same. A horrible dread was building inside her as he got quieter and quieter. "Come on," she said. "I'll drive."

SHE SPED DOWN the highway in the dark, her heart in her throat as Paul made call after call.

First, he called Cy.

"He's taken my niece," he said.

"I'm on my way," Cy said, and hung up with a click.

The second call was to the director of the FBI.

"Edenhurst, it's Harrison," he said, his voice tense. "There's a serial killer in Northern California. A journalist friend of mine stumbled onto his trail. She brought me in to help. And now he's realized we're onto him. He's taken my niece. I need every resource in Northern California, Nevada, and Oregon at my disposal. Can you make that happen?"

He listened for a second. "Thank you. I'll keep you updated." He paused, listening again, his jaw working. "I'll try, sir," he said, and this time, his voice broke.

Abby reached over, squeezing his thigh reassuringly as he hung up, dialing another number.

As she drove, he made fifteen calls. From governors, to state reps, to the head of the highway patrol.

They were ten miles outside of Castella Rock by the time he finally put the phone down. He couldn't seem to sit still, his fingers tapping against his knee, like they were itching for a trigger to pull and a man to aim a gun at.

She didn't know what to say. *It's going to be okay?* But what if it wasn't? *I'm sorry?* Because she was.

Had her snooping tipped Cass's killer off? Had he been watching her this whole time?

He must've chosen Robin for a reason—it was too much of a coincidence that he'd taken the niece of the man who was now hunting him.

God, she *had* done this. This was her fault. If anything happened to Robin . . .

She felt like pulling over and throwing up. She'd known Robin her entire life. She'd watched her wobble up the steps of the orchard house as a toddler, woven daisy wreaths for her hair when she was a flower girl in her aunt Faye's wedding. At the barbecue this week, she'd just promised to help her on her college essays. The girl had the world at her fingertips.

She'd be damned if that bastard took her away like he did Cass.

"Nothing is going to happen to her," she said, out loud, to make it real, for herself and for him.

"Something already has happened to her,"

Paul said, and the resignation in his voice, the brokenness stole her breath for a moment.

She pulled off the highway, taking a left on Main Street, heading toward Georgia's house. She parked across the street from it, and turned to him, all the resolve she felt in her face.

"We can do this. We're going to get her back."

"Abby, I can't make those promises," he said. "Not to my sister. Not when . . ." He stopped, staring down at his hands for a moment, and then finally, when he'd gathered himself, said, "I can't make those promises, with who I am. With what I do. You know what happens, when you promise to bring a parent's child home safe, and then you don't?"

"It won't be that way," Abby said. "I won't let it."

He smiled, and it was a sad smile, a loving smile, a fond smile. He reached out, stroking a thumb over skin, following the constellation of freckles sweeping over the arc of her cheekbone. "You've always been so stubborn," he said. "But we can't promise them, Abby. All we can do is tell them what they already know."

"What do you mean?"

"We tell them that Robin is a fighter," he said. "In body, in mind, and in spirit. We tell them that she is smart and she is skilled. She will be looking to escape. She will take whatever out she has to. And we won't tell them that this kind of spirit? This kind of strength? It's likely going to get her killed unless I find her first."

Abby felt like she'd been punched, and she knew the words were meant to knock the air out of her. He was telling it to her straight. Giving her a glimpse of what his world was like. God, how hard the last years must've been for him, alone, no one to share this with.

She lifted her chin. "Okay," she said. "Then let's go find her first."

GEORGIA AND JASON'S house was one of the nicer in town, but right now, it felt like a morgue as they walked inside. Tandy, Paul's mother, opened the door when they knocked on it. When she met her only son's eyes, the woman, who was built like steel with a heart to match, seemed to crumble.

"Paul," she said, tears filling her eyes. "What do we do?"

"Where's Georgia?" he asked.

"She collapsed," said Faye, coming into the foyer. Her mouth was tense, but her eyes were clear, which made Abby feel slightly more assured. Faye was a tough cookie. She'd be the calming influence here. "She's upstairs with Rose and Jason."

"I need to talk to her," Paul said.

"Why don't we go and fix something to eat?" Abby asked Tandy and Faye, taking Paul's hint. "We all need to keep our strength up. Where are the rest of the kids?"

"My kids are with their dad," Faye said. "I haven't told them. I haven't even called Mara. You know how reception is over there even when she isn't operating. I . . . I don't know what to say."

"We'll figure it out," Tandy assured her daughter.

The older woman looked over at the kitchen, her gray eyebrows knitting together like she'd never been in one before.

"Let's sit down first," Abby suggested, and Tandy seemed grateful for the guidance.

"I don't understand how this happened," she said. "There are people all over those meets. How did no one see her?"

"Have you talked to people who were there?" Abby asked. "What about the boys on her wrestling team?"

"The deputies are questioning everyone," Tandy said. "But the sheriff said we couldn't issue a missing person report!"

"Don't worry, Paul will take care of that," Abby assured her. "He was on the phone all the way here. He must have called at least a dozen different people. Everyone is looking for Robin. They'll find her."

"I don't . . . I don't understand why anyone would want to do this," Tandy said, baffled. "Things like this don't happen here."

Faye looked over her mother's head at Abby and she knew they were thinking the same thing. That Castella Rock was a lot of things, but sweet, safe small town it wasn't.

Things like this happened here, because things like this happened *everywhere*.

There were footsteps on the stairs. Abby got up, hurrying out of the living room to meet Paul at the stairs.

"Is Georgia okay?"

Paul shook his head.

"Paul, what do we do?" she asked.

"We need to go," he said.

"Where?" she asked, but then he looked at her, a grim sort of foreboding in his eyes, and she knew.

It was time to go back to the Doctor.

CHAPTER 28

"Where the hell is he?"

Paul burst through the doors of the prison like a tornado, Abby chasing behind him. The intake guard's eyes widened when he took in Paul's wild look.

"Special Agent Harrison," Paul ground out, clearly barely keeping his voice under control. "Director Edenhurst called ahead. Take us to see Howard Wells. Immediately."

"Right away, sir," the guard stuttered, hitting the button that opened the armed door.

"You need to stay calm," Abby said under her breath as they walked through the metal detectors and got patted down. A muscle ticked in his jaw, and he yanked his hand through his hair, slicking it off his forehead with an impatient movement. "He'll use it against you if you're this visibly upset," she said. "I know him better than you. I've studied him."

"I have this under control, Abby," he said, as she watched him out of the corner of her eye worriedly.

"Ms. Winthrop, you're back," said a voice.

Abby turned to see Stan, the guard from her last visit, standing there.

"Hi, Stan," she said. "Yes, I'm back. Can you please take us to see Wells?"

"Now," Paul ground out.

Stan's eyes widened slightly as he took in Paul's tense shoulders and the anger radiating off him. "Will do," he said.

"Stay close to me," Paul said, as Stan began to lead them through the block. Even this early in the morning, the hooting and hollering rose to a din. With each step, Paul grew tenser and tenser, a gleam she'd never seen in his eyes as he stared down the bolder inmates.

By the time Stan got them across the prison and into the wing that held the solitary confinement cells, Paul was practically vibrating. Abby reached out, settling a palm between his shoulders, trying to soothe him somehow, but it was no use.

He was operating on pure feral instinct. Protect his family. At any cost.

Stan led them down the long hall, toward the door at the end, where Wells's lonely cell lay. As he reached the last door, Abby turned to Paul and said, "Remember what I said."

He nodded curtly as Stan unlocked the last door, ushering them inside.

The lights flicked on, and Paul stalked over to the Plexiglas wall that separated them from the serial killer.

"Well, isn't this a surprise." Wells unfolded himself from his bed. "And look at me, so underdressed." He grinned at Abby, wiggling his fingers at her, clearly enjoying his range of movement.

They hadn't had time to put him in a straitjacket. She bit the inside of her lip, telling herself that the way her heart picked up was stupid. He couldn't get to her in there.

"Who's your friend, Abigail?" Wells asked, his eyes glittering as he took Paul in. Abby didn't say anything. There was no way in hell Wells didn't know who Paul was, after all these years.

"He's quite the specimen, isn't he?" Wells asked. "He looks positively . . . all-American."

Only Wells could make that sound like an insult. Like something base and disgusting.

"Where is he?" Paul demanded.

Wells smirked. "I don't know who you're talking about."

Paul's eyes narrowed, his shoulders tensing.

"Okay, you want to play that game?" he asked. "Then I'm gonna tell you a story, Wells." He sat down on the bench in front of his cell, leaning forward on his elbows, eyes glittering in a way Abby had never seen. "It's the story of two men who somehow found a commonality in each other. A sick, twisted, violent commonality, but still, finding someone *like* you? That's a powerful thing. You couldn't resist, when you found him, could you? He was like murderous clay you could mold. Your perfect creation. Except . . . he wasn't content with that, was he? He wanted something more. He wanted something different."

Abby shivered as Paul leaned forward and Wells's smirk twitched, just a bit.

"Your student outgrew you," Paul said, each word a deadly barb that made Wells's eyes flare. "He evolved beyond his teacher. He wasn't content to just take the girls and kill them. No, he wanted *more*. He wanted to keep them. To draw it out. And you didn't like that. You, you're about that moment, Howard, when your hands slip around their throats, and the light starts to fade from their eyes. That's what gets you off. And desecrating their bodies after. But you never cut them when they were alive. You weren't into pain. You're into the power. And your boy? Your student? He's into it for the challenge. It's about the competition. First, it was a game between you and him. But he won that. And now? It's him versus the girl. How long can he keep her alive? How long can he keep her captive? How many girls can he take before someone catches on? It's the ultimate competition. It's not even really him versus the girl. It's him versus the world."

A sharklike smile spread across Wells's face. "I see you're not just a pretty face," he drawled. "But neither am I. Are you familiar with the tale of Hercules and Antaeus, Agent Harrison?" Wells asked. "It's much like the Achilles myth. A little lesser known, I suppose. I won't bore you with the details. Just the lesson. I do so love a lesson."

Abby's face was like stone as Wells's eyes flicked to her, then back to Paul.

"Antaeus was thought to be invincible," Wells said. "But he had one weakness. Hercules found it. And he used it. You can guess who was left standing."

"Are you casting yourself as Antaeus in this scenario?" Paul asked. "And your protégé as Hercules? That's quite the pedestal to put him on."

Wells laughed. "Oh, my dear boy. I'm not *either*." He spread his arms wide. "If I'm anyone, I'm Zeus himself. *You* are Antaeus here, Agent Harrison."

Wells's eyes flicked back to Abby. "I found your weakness. I can hardly blame you. She's a sly, fiery thing. Like a fox. She wanted to run, and I lured her right into my trap." His smile curled around his lips and Abby was unable to stop the shudder that overtook her body.

Paul didn't react. He merely raised an eyebrow, waiting for Wells to continue.

"I've wanted to meet you for a long time," Wells said. "But I knew you wouldn't come," Wells said. "Not unless I finally gave Abby what she wanted."

"And why did you want to see me?" Paul asked.

"Because I've made a lot of things in my life," Wells said. "I've created some damn good surgeons. Even a few decent coroners. I am the kind of teacher who truly transforms lives. I thought my crowning achievement was my protégé. But then . . ." His grin widened, terrifying, a shark in the water, smelling blood for the first time. "Then I created an FBI agent," he said, a delighted chuckle wrapping around Abby like a snake. "And not just *any* FBI Agent. Special Supervisory Agent Paul Harrison." He lowered his voice as he rattled Paul's title off. "The agency's golden boy. There's talk that you're on track for assistant director before you're forty. There's even rumblings of a congressional campaign, if you don't set your sights on director. And the choices I made set you on that path. Isn't life grand, sometimes?"

Abby wanted to reach forward and tear that pleased look on his face off. He had *nothing* to do with Paul's successes. How dare he. Anger sparked, hot and low in her body, and she could feel it spreading to her cheeks.

But Paul's face didn't even ripple at Wells's outrageous claims. "You had nothing to do with why I became an FBI agent," he said.

"Don't insult my intelligence, Paul," Wells tutted. "You were headed for a baseball career before Cass's murder. And then all of a sudden you were done with baseball and applying for colleges and aiming your sights on Quantico. I did that. I suppose my protégé did have a hand in it, since he did the actual killing. But you didn't know that, did you? You thought it was me. I was the one you saw when you closed your eyes at night. When you were at Quantico, it was my face you imagined when you fired your gun at those paper targets. I formed you into the kind of man who could be a hero."

"You don't get to take credit for what I built from the ashes," Paul said, the resolve in his face making her stomach twist. "You think that you and your boy, whoever the hell he is, are the most horrible thing that's ever happened to me, Wells?" He let out a short bark of a laugh that hurt Abby to hear. "Sorry to disappoint, but you two barely make it to the top five. You want to talk about transforming life experiences? Let's talk about the man who strapped enough C4 to me to blow me, himself, the little girl and the cabin we were in to kingdom come. Let's talk about my father dying forty years too early because even though he got sober, it wasn't soon enough and his liver failed. Let's talk about what it's like, to have a six-year-old girl die in your arms because her father shot her entire family and then himself. You want to talk *horror* with me, Wells? You want to talk *evil*? You're a sick fuck deluded by his own phony murderous grandeur. You're not even the most interesting serial killer I've come up against."

Abby had never wanted to reach for him so much in her life. She knew she couldn't, that Wells would just delight in this show of affection and worry, but it was hard to stop herself, when Paul was laying out his truths so fiercely, lobbing them like grenades at Wells to show he had no power over him.

"You wanna really see what kind of man I am?" Paul asked, rising to his feet. "Abby, you should leave."

Abby's eyes widened. What the hell was he going to do? "No way."

"Fine." Paul looked over at Stan. "Let him out," he demanded.

Stan gaped at him. "What?" he sputtered.

"You heard me," Paul said. "Open the God-damn door."

Stan backed away. "No," he said.

"Paul—" Abby started to stay, but then faded off in shock as Paul strode over and without a hint of hesitation, snatched the keys off the chain on Stan's belt.

"You can't do that!" Stan shouted as Paul slotted the key into the lock. He hurried across the room, slamming down on the emergency button, and then ran out of the room, leaving the two of them alone.

"Paul," Abby said again.

"Leave," he said.

"I am not leaving you alone to kill him!" she snapped and Wells shrieked with laughter as

Paul turned the key in the lock and jerked the door open.

Abby's fingers curled into fists, her entire body screamed at her to *run* as Paul grabbed Wells by the neck and shoved him against the Plexiglas wall of his cell. But instead of beginning to pummel him, he grabbed a chunk of Wells's hair and tore it out. Keeping one elbow on his neck and holding him pinned, he dug in his other pocket for a small plastic evidence bag, depositing the hair into it.

"This is what kind of man I am," he hissed in Wells's ear, shoving the bag in his face like a taunt. "The kind of man who trusts in science. In the law and justice. And in my people's ability to outsmart you and your protégé. Just you wait, Wells. Your boy's gonna be in the cell across from yours any day now."

He jerked away from him, and the man panted against the glass, dazed and red-faced, as Paul stepped out of the cell and locked the door.

Abby stared at him, wide-eyed and breathless. "I thought you were going to kill him," she said.

"He doesn't have the guts!" Wells shouted.

Paul shot him a disgusted look. "You're not worth the energy or the bullet."

Without another word, he took Abby's hand,

and led her out of the room, where they were greeted by a crowd of guards, led by Stan, looking panicked and worried.

Paul tossed Stan his keys. "He's all yours, boys."

CHAPTER 29

When they got back to the farmhouse, Paul tossed the bag of Wells's hair to Zooey.

"You make sure it was from the root?" she asked. "I need the root."

"It's from the root," he said.

"Good."

"Why are you testing his hair?" Abby asked. Her stomach leapt, horror filling her. "You didn't . . . you didn't dig Cass up, did you?"

"No," Zooey assured her. "I have a theory. It's kind of a wild theory, but after I talked it through with our profiler in DC, I figured it was worth a shot."

"Zooey thinks that Wells and the unsub could be related," Paul explained.

"What?" Shock coursed through Abby. "Seriously?"

"I kept asking myself, why is Wells protecting this guy? He's too much of a control freak to trust all his secrets—his *teachings*—to someone who was on the other side of an anonymous screen. They may have communicated online, but they had to know each other in real life. So what kind of bond keeps Wells from giving him up, even after he framed him for murder?

"Wells's first wife, Ruth, left him after only a year of marriage," Zooey said. "She didn't go directly back to her family, even though that was her original plan. She went to stay with an aunt. And six months later, she shows up at the hospital, pregnant. The thing is, she doesn't leave with a baby."

"She gave the baby up for adoption," Abby said in realization. "Oh, that must have *infuriated* him. He's obsessed with legacy."

"What better way to insure your legacy than to track your son down and teach him your serial killer ways?" Zooey asked.

It was a chilling thought. Twisted. But it would make sense of the fact that Wells never exposed his protégé. It never sat right with Abby that he'd kept quiet about it, all these years.

"It might explain the animosity the unsub clearly feels against Wells," Paul said. "He dedicated a lot to framing him. But I'm guessing that the high of that faded fast."

"Which is why he was back to not just killing girls, but abducting them and keeping them captive in just twenty-four months," Abby finished, feeling grim.

"Exactly," Paul said.

"I'm gonna take this to the sheriff's station," Zooey said. "My equipment got delivered this morning. I should have the relevant DNA strands isolated and run through the database in a few hours. If our guy's ever been arrested, we should get a hit."

"And then we find Robin," Paul said.

Abby reached out and squeezed his shoulder.

"I need to get back to my mom's," Paul said. "Georgia is . . . she's not well. And Jason's barely keeping it together."

"Of course," Abby said. "I'll go with you—" she started to say, but there was a knock at her door.

"Abby?" called a voice. "I've got the monthly yield reports."

That was Jonah, her orchard manager. "Go on," she told Paul. "I've got to deal with orchard stuff. I'll come over later and bring everyone food."

He reached out, grabbing her hand and squeezing it briefly. "Thanks, Winny."

She smiled at the nickname. "I want to do everything I can," she said. "For all of you."

"I know," he said. "It just . . . it means a lot."

"Hey, Abby!"

She turned toward Jonah's voice. "Coming," she called. "Go," she urged Paul. "Zooey, you'll call us if you get a hit on the DNA?"

"Will do," Zooey said, gathering her bag up and plopping the enormous hot-pink sun hat she had come in with on her head. "It's gonna be okay, boss," she told him. "I'm gonna beat these jerks with science. Just you wait."

Abby hurried out to meet Jonah, who had a big stack of ledgers in his hands and a smile when he saw her and Paul.

"Jonah, man, I hadn't realized you were working for Abby now," Paul said, holding his hand out and taking the shorter man's, shaking it warmly. "She's treating you all right, I hope?"

"She's a great boss," Jonah said. "I was so sorry to hear about Robin, Paul. The whole church is praying for her and your entire family."

"Thank you," Paul said. "We appreciate those prayers. I've gotta go. I'll leave you to your business. Abby, call me if anything changes, okay?"

She nodded, watching him leave, wishing like anything she could follow him.

But life didn't stop, and she'd been putting Jonah off for weeks.

"Come on into the living room," she said with a smile. "You want something to drink?"

FOUR HOURS LATER, the monthly yields and budgets had been recorded and typed into the spreadsheets, thanks to Jonah's meticulous record-keeping.

"You really are great at this, Jonah," Abby said, shutting the ledger. She got up, stretching her arms over her head. "How's Maria doing?" she asked, referring to his wife, who owned the diner in town.

"Great," he said. "Diner's busier than ever."

"That's great," she said. Speaking of food . . . it was getting late. And Roscoe hadn't whined for food in hours, even though it was past his dinnertime. Frowning, she whistled, but didn't hear the click of his paws against the hardwood.

"Roscoe!" she called.

"He wander off again?" Jonah asked. "I swear, that dog's getting senile." He got up and went to the front door, calling for him.

But there was no response.

Getting worried—Roscoe wasn't one to miss *any* meal—Abby shoved her feet into her yellow mucking-around boots and went out onto the porch. "Roscoe!" she yelled into the fading light. The sun was setting fast beyond the trees and the dog was nowhere to be found.

"I'm gonna go look for him," she told Jonah.

"I'll check out the barn," Jonah said.

They parted, Jonah heading west and Abby heading east, toward the trees.

"Roscoe!" she called, her heart squeezing in her chest. Where was that smelly beast? If anything happened to him . . .

She didn't need any more losses right now. She knew it was silly, especially with what was going on, but Roscoe was the last dog her dad ever had. He'd slept at the foot of her father's bed every night, the entire time he was sick.

Her father had been a hard man, but his gentleness had always come out with animals. And sometimes, Abby would cling to that thought.

"Roscoe! Come on, boy! Mama has treats!" she called, wishing she'd thought to grab a bag of chips or something from the kitchen.

She heard the crack of a branch behind her. Was that him?

"Roscoe?"

Another crack. Footsteps. Coming at her fast. Running.

Jonah wouldn't be running. It was a flash of a thought, her stomach leapt and she turned— just a second too late.

Something smashed into the side of her head. Pain lanced against her skull, it felt like it was splitting in two, and something warm trickled down her forehead as she fell to the ground.

The last thing she saw, before her eyes fluttered shut and darkness overtook her, were the branches of the trees and the green of their leaves.

CHAPTER 30

Two hours earlier

"It's going to be okay, Georgia," Rose said soothingly, smoothing her sister's hair off her forehead like she was a child.

Georgia didn't even react. His sister's normally bright eyes were dull, and the whites threaded with red. Someone had suggested giving her a Xanax, but Jason had shaken his head curtly.

His brother-in-law looked like he was fighting the urge to cry at every second. Paul had tried to talk to him earlier, but Jason had finally made him stop, shaking his head.

"I'm gonna lose it, man," he'd told Paul. "And I can't. Because Georgia and Robin need me. So just . . . tell me what I need to do."

"You're doing it," Paul assured him. "Your job is to take care of Georgia. My job is to get Robin back."

Jason had nodded, his face had crumpled, and Paul had wished to God he had the rest of his team here because he was usually good with victims' families, but this was *his* family being victimized. He was no good at this. There were no rules for this. No handbook. No protocol.

There was just him. And everyone expected him to come through. And if he didn't?

He couldn't even think about what would happen—how it would break everyone—if he didn't bring Robin home, safe and sound.

He was going to tear that man apart with his bare hands. And no one was going to stop him.

Rules had served him well for many years. But now? He would break every one to bring Robin home safe and whole to his family. Nothing else mattered.

He stepped out of the bedroom where his sisters were soothing Georgia, knowing they were much better at it than he was. His mother was making her way up the stairs with a tray of food. There were circles under her eyes that hadn't been there at the start of the week and a tightness around her mouth that he remembered from the days before his dad got sober.

"How's she doing?" she asked.

Paul shook his head.

"How could this happen?" his mother asked, looking at him like he had the answer.

He didn't want to tell her the truth. That this likely happened because of him. That the bastard had taken Robin because he'd gotten involved.

"I am going to get her back, Mom," he said, the promise in his voice ringing out, true and clear.

"I know you are," she said. "I know, sweetheart."

"Mom?" one of his sisters called from the room.

His mother sniffed, her eyes bright. "I need to bring this to them," she said. "They need to eat."

"Of course," he said, stepping out of her way.

"Come sit with us," she said.

But his phone had started ringing in his pocket. "I've got to take this," he said, seeing that it was Cy.

He hurried down the stairs and onto the porch, where it was quiet and private. It felt like the entire orchard house was full of people—Pastor Jamison was in the living room with a whole slew of teenagers who must be Robin's friends. Even the boys—especially a group of them in the back—had red eyes.

"Hey, Cy, what's up?" he asked.

"You said you were looking for seven missing girls, right?" Cy asked.

"That's right," Paul said.

"Then I think you need to come out here."

Paul frowned. There was a chilling note in Cy's voice, and he wasn't the kind of man who was easily ruffled. "Where are you?"

"I'm out in the Siskiyous, about forty miles in past mile marker 704," Cyrus said. "Some firefighter buddies of mine just finished putting out the latest fire that firebug the sheriff's chasing set. They came across something really strange out past McCloud, pretty deep in the backwoods, and called me in immediately. You need to see it. And you need to bring that pink-haired scientist of yours. Because I'm pretty sure I'm looking at a mass grave here, Paul."

A chill went through him. Cyrus was not someone who leapt to conclusions. He'd traveled all around the globe—and he knew he had experience with horrors like mass graves.

Had he found their unsub's burial ground?

"How do I get to you?" Paul asked. "Zooey and I are on our way."

CHAPTER 31

The Siskiyou Mountains are a place of staggering beauty—and staggering secrets. The dense forest that takes up a large chunk of Northern California and Oregon is the home of a lot of good people, quite a few shady characters, and more dead bodies than anyone would like to admit.

There were places in these mountains that hadn't been walked by a person in decades, mines that had fallen into disuse after technology had finally sped up and the railroad went bust, and old roads that hadn't been taken care of in years. After all, there was no one to walk them.

"This is unbelievable," Zooey said, staring numbly out at the valley stretched in front of them. There was still the scent of smoke in the air, and she could almost feel the heat still coming off the ground.

They were eighty miles into the forest, far from people, from homes, from any towns. This was the real wilderness: hard to access, hard to find. The small clearing that Cyrus's firefighter friends had discovered during the final run of the mountain was not natural. It was man-made.

Their unsub had cleared these trees. By himself. One by one. To create the perfect burial ground.

There were seven Xs formed by volcanic stones laid out in the valley, marking each grave with a six-foot mark. Like a sick imitation of a headstone, but instead of the girl's names, instead of giving them personhood, instead of honoring them, he rendered them nameless, voiceless.

Like things instead of humans.

Paul stared across the clearing. The floodlights had been set up and a forensic team from Sacramento was twenty minutes away, choppered in by special request.

Zooey was going to need some help.

"I'm going in," she declared. Without another word, she marched up to the first X, pulling on a pair of latex gloves, and then a pair of leather work gloves over it. The group of firefighters Cy had convinced to stick behind and help gathered around her as she began to describe what she needed them to do with the rocks.

"You think this is gonna help find him?" Cy

asked, coming up to stand next to Paul. "Or do you think this is just gonna really piss him off?"

It was a thought that he hadn't wanted to voice, but there Cy went, being the blunt weapon to his more careful approach. It was why the two of them were friends. And why he really was the only person he'd trust with this.

"I'm pretty sure this is going to do both," Paul said. "Look at this place." He gestured around them. "This is his temple. As far as he's concerned, he built this. He probably comes here to visit them regularly. You don't bury them like this, with care, with markers, if you're not coming to see them."

"You should have the sheriff do armed patrols around the perimeter, so your pack of geeks flying in don't get picked off one by one," Cyrus said. "He's gonna come back here and see what you've done."

"I know," Paul said. "We'll make sure they're protected."

"You're gambling a lot here, Paul," Cyrus warned. "He's got your niece."

"I know that," he said, his words coming out harsh. "You think I don't know that? You think I don't know what's at stake here? But this guy . . . he's had almost sixteen years to evolve, Cyrus. Do you know what kind of ego you've gotta have to take a girl and not just kill her, but keep her captive for months, maybe *years*? That's a damn hard shell of confidence to penetrate. The only way he slips up is if it feels like someone's finally pierced his shield. This . . ." He gestured to Zooey and the firefighters, who were making great time with moving the rocks off the first grave. "This is my arrow into his seemingly invincible armor. First cut's always the deepest."

"I hope you're right," Cyrus said.

"I've gotta be."

By THE TIME the team of forensic techs had arrived, the sheriff and his deputies had also arrived. And Zooey had started digging. The firefighters had moved on to the second grave under Zooey's careful instructions as the forensic techs had gathered around her, awaiting instructions.

"Boss!"

Paul hurried over, steeling himself when he saw Zooey had uncovered the first body. His fists clenched when he recognized Keira Rice. And his stomach churned when he saw her hair, French-braided carefully along her skull, her plaits tucked over her shoulders, tied on each end with bright yellow ribbons.

Just like how Cass used to wear in her hair

when she played softball. Down to the bows on each end.

He was duplicating her. Because he didn't get to kill her the way *he* wanted. *Fuck*. It was so sick. It made him want to find a tree and punch his fists raw and bloody.

"Goddamn it," he said. He'd hoped that maybe, Keira was alive still. Even though he knew deep down that it was unlikely.

"She looks like she's only been dead for days," Zooey said. "Hey, you." She snapped her fingers at one of the forensic techs. "Go get one of the deputies. I'm going to need a body bag and a stretcher to carry the bodies up the embankment."

She leaned back on her heels, staring at Keira's body. "Poor girl," she whispered, her eyes sad. But then she lifted them to Paul's, her expression turning determined. "If there's anything to find, boss, I'll find it. We'll bring Robin back and catch this bastard. He can outsmart a lot of things, but he can't outsmart science."

"Paul!" Sheriff Alan hurried down the slope that led into the clearing, a satellite phone in his hand. "Your mama's trying to reach you. Station says she's been calling nonstop."

Paul frowned, taking the sat phone from the sheriff and hitting the receive button.

"Mom?"

"Paul? Oh, thank God. Where *are you*? I've been calling everywhere trying to find you."

"I'm at a crime scene, Mom. What's wrong?"

"Abby's gone, Paul," his mother babbled, her voice shaky. "She was looking for the dog with Jonah. Jonah's got a concussion. He said he didn't even see who hit him. And when he came to, she was gone. He can't find her. I can't find her. Everyone's looking and no one can find her."

Paul's hand clenched around the sat phone, his entire fucking world coming to a freezing stop.

He'd taken Robin.

And now, he'd taken Abby.

Of course.

He was still evolving.

Still challenging himself.

He needed to prove he was better than Wells.

And two captives were better than one.

CHAPTER 32

"Abby! Abby! Come on, wake up!"

Someone was tapping lightly on her face, well, more like slapping her face.

"Please, Abby! I really need you to wake up."

She blinked. God, her head was killing her. She tried to swallow, and her mouth was so dry she sputtered, her tongue feeling like a wad of dry cotton in her mouth. Her vision swam, blurry and indistinct, until the brown-and-cream blur looming over her came into focus.

"Robin," she croaked out, trying to sit up too fast and nearly throwing up in the process. The world flipped upside down and tilted, the rough brown walls of the . . . where *were* they?

"Sit up slow," Robin encouraged her. "Whatever he gives you makes you feel like crap at first. But it wears off quick."

The teenager helped Abby sit up, leaning against one of the wood walls of the room—no, it was a shed. A windowless one. There was a stinking bucket in the corner and a thin, bare mattress against the far wall.

And a giant, brown-red stain on the concrete floor.

Abby sucked in a sharp breath, staring at the stain. Robin's eyes flew to the spot and the girl's throat clicked as she swallowed.

"I know," she said. "Don't look at it. Abby, did you see who took you?"

Abby's eyes widened. "You haven't seen him?" He'd had Robin for two days. Surely she'd seen *something* in that time. How were they going to get out of here?

Robin shook her head, pointing to the steel door, which had what looked like a flap welded to the bottom. "He shoves food through there twice a day."

"What happened, Robin?" Abby asked. "What can you remember?"

"I was at the meet," Robin said. "I'd finished my match and went into the girls' locker room. It was totally empty because I'm the only girl on the team. I was going to shower, but I got really dizzy all of a sudden. And the next thing I know, I'm here. I think I got dosed."

Panic soared through Abby, and she was trying hard not to let it show on her face. She needed to stay calm, for Robin's sake. She was the adult here. The last thing the poor girl needed was an adult freaking out just as much as she was.

They needed to work together to get out of here. They both needed to stay calm and collected.

And strong.

"Do you remember drinking or eating anything different?" Abby asked. "Did someone you didn't know give you a drink?"

Robin shook her head. "I'm really anal about my water bottle," she said. "I do these thirst-quencher mixes of grapefruit juice, water, and Gatorade."

He could've slipped anything in her drink and she probably wouldn't have noticed the taste. Crap.

"I didn't have my bottle on me the whole time," Robin admitted. "I didn't think I needed to watch it. That was stupid of me."

"No, it wasn't, sweetie," Abby said, reaching out and hugging her. "This isn't your fault," she said, looking around the shed, trying to see if there was *any* way out. It was maybe ten feet across, and about the same wide. There was nothing in the shed but the mattress and the bucket, but Abby could see marks along the far wall.

Someone clawing at the wood, trying to get out.

She wanted to shake and cry and scream. But she couldn't. She steeled herself, she pushed it down, the terror, the rising fear, the question of *what the hell will become of us?*

She wasn't going to let what happened to Cass, what happened to Keira Rice, what happened to all the other lost girls, happen to Robin.

She was putting an end to this. An end to *him.* Starting now.

"Robin," she said, pulling away from her, looking at her seriously. Robin's lip trembled, her eyes filling with tears. "We're going to get out of this," she told her, believing every word. "We are going to get home. Both of us. I want you to tell me *everything* about the last two days. And then we're going to make a plan."

CHAPTER 33

As one of the sheriff's deputies drove him off the mountain and raced toward town, Paul did the thing he should have done from the start: he called Agent Grace Sinclair.

"I just came in from my trafficking case," she said, in lieu of a hello. "I got an illuminating email from Zooey. It seems you've been taking a working vacation. What's the news on your niece?"

"No sign," Paul said. "And now he's taken Abby."

"Your journalist friend?" Grace asked. "Shit. He's spiraling. Tell me everything," she directed.

"I think it started out a typical teacher/student dynamic," Paul said. "Somehow, Howard Wells found a protégé . . . someone he felt he could mold into the perfect killer. And then that perfect killer rebelled."

"The student outpaced the master," Grace

said. "That's not a submissive personality. It means he was dominant from the start, Dr. X just didn't recognize it, or he was hiding it."

"He seems to have a talent for hiding in plain sight," Paul said.

"Highly intelligent and highly manipulative is *not* a good combination, Paul."

"I know, Grace," he said. "I've found his burial ground. Zooey's digging up seven girls' bodies right now."

He could practically hear her gritting her teeth through the phone. "Zooey's email said you went to see Dr. X at the prison," Grace said. "What did he say?"

"He seems to be under the impression he created me," Paul snorted. "Typical delusions of grandeur. Thinks he set me on my path. Wants to take credit for me. Talked a bunch about some Greek myth."

"Which myth?"

"Um, some guy who fought Hercules and lost," Paul said.

"Antaeus the giant?" Grace asked.

"Yeah, that was it."

"Hmm," Grace said.

"What?" Paul asked.

"It's just kind of an obscure myth," Grace said. "It's part of Hercules's larger story, but it's just kind of a small part of it. Was he comparing himself to Hercules?"

"No, he said *I* was Antaeus. That my weakness . . ." It hit him all at once. "He said my weakness was Abby."

"Why would he . . . *oh!*" Grace said, in realization.

"I can't talk about it right now," Paul said. Not when Abby was missing, locked up somewhere with Robin. God, he hoped the two of them were together. Abby would protect Robin with her life, and he was so damned grateful for that, grateful that she was that person.

Grateful that he loved someone like that.

She would die fighting for Robin if she had to. He just had to make sure it didn't come to that.

"Okay, but how would X's apprentice know to go after Abby?" Grace asked.

"She visited Wells in prison last week," Paul said. "She's been trying to get him to see her for months. That's how this all got started. He finally agreed to see her. She went in there and told him she knew he hadn't killed Cassandra Martin. And he messed up—he said something that confirmed her suspicions."

"But in Zooey's email, she says that you initially thought the unsub was the deputy," Grace said. "Ryan. And it turned out he wasn't. Your unsub killed him before Abby could get to him. So my question is: How did the unsub know Abby was looking into Ryan? Or *anyone* for that matter? How did he even know she was onto him?"

Paul blinked, thinking. How *had* the unsub known to kill Ryan Clay?

"Wells," he breathed in realization. "Wells and the unsub are still communicating somehow."

"I'd bet my art collection on it," Grace said grimly. "Get Zooey on how they're communicating. Gavin and I will work with our people in DC to get the prison warden in line."

"Thank you, Grace." Sometimes he needed to talk things out to really see the full picture, and she was always the best at that.

"Find out how they're communicating," Grace said. "You'll find him. And your niece. And Abby. You can do this, Paul."

He knew she was right.

She had to be.

WHEN HE CALLED Zooey with the news, she'd been furious that she hadn't made the leap herself. "What is wrong with me?!" she had demanded over the phone, something Paul wisely didn't answer. After leaving Cyrus with strict orders to "watch those techs like a hawk, don't let them damage my evidence!" she'd hopped on the helicopter and had almost beaten Paul to the tiny office in the sheriff's station that she'd set up as her lab.

Now she had four computers set up next to each other on a steel table and two more laptops rigged up behind her, running a complicated code that Paul had no clue about.

"God, the prison's security grid is like Silly Putty," Zooey muttered, tapping frantically on the keyboard. "Okay, searching through every email sent on their network now."

"Hey, do a search," Paul said. "For *Antaeus* and *Hercules*."

"From the myth?" Zooey asked, frowning.

"Wells brought it up when I saw him," Paul explained. "Grace thought it might be important."

Zooey typed the names in, hitting the enter button, but nothing came up. "Nada," she said. Then her eyes lit up. "But wait a second." She pushed her chair down the table, to the last of the computers, beginning to type. "I wonder . . ." she muttered to herself. "Oh, my God!" She jerked in her seat. "Boss! You're a genius! Well, you *and* Abby!"

"What?" Paul said, hurrying over to her.

"One of Abby's theories was that maybe Dr. X

and his apprentice met online. Apparently Wells liked Craigslist, so that was one of the possibilities she floated. Look what happens when I run a special search algorithm I created for past and present Craigslist postings and add word *Antaeus* to the search terms . . ."

Posts began to appear on the screen, one after another.

"This one looks like the first one, dated right after Cass was killed and Wells was caught." Zooey pointed at the screen.

"'My dear Paeon,'" Paul read. "'Have you learned your lesson? Yours truly, Antaeus.'"

"This one's dated around the time Ramona Quinn disappeared. 'My dear Paeon,'" Zooey read, moving on to the second. "'The Harvest has arrived, and what a bounty! It's such a pity you aren't here to share it with me. The fruit is so ripe, so ready to be plucked.'" She made a face. "Is he . . . is he talking about the girls?" she asked Paul.

Paul felt about as sick as she looked. "I think so," he said quietly. "Look at this one: 'My dear Paeon, It is so hard saying goodbye. Sometimes I wonder if your way is better: plucking the fruit before it's ready. I suppose I cannot blame your crude, base palate. Sometimes unripened fruit can be sweet. But I prefer to ripen the fruit myself, I take such gentle care until the fruit is just so sweet. You really can't go back after you've tried it my way. Yours truly, Antaeus.'"

"Fuck, that's creepy," Paul said. "The other name. Paeon. What does that mean?"

"He was the physician to the Greek gods," Zooey said.

Well, that made sense. "Of course he was. See if there are any from Wells, under the name Paeon. He's gotta be reading these letters from our unsub. Is he answering them?"

Zooey ran a second search. "There's only one," she said. "Dated the day Abby went to see Wells the first time."

Paul looked at the letter.

Antaeus—
A sweet little fox visited last week. I sent her your way.
Happy hunting, my young protégé.
This time, the lesson to be learned is yours.

—Paeon

His stomach clenched. Wells had compared Abby to a fox when they'd seen each other. He'd sicced his fucking protégé on Abby. Practically served her up on a silver platter.

Abby was Wells's final lesson to his protégé: a woman with more nerve than she knew what to do with and a determination that didn't quit.

She was his worst nightmare.

He would see her as his greatest challenge.

"Find a way to trace this shit," he gritted out to Zooey. "I need some air."

CHAPTER 34

So he brings food before it gets dark," Abby said.

She'd been drilling Robin for the past three hours, trying to get an idea of the schedule their captor was on. They needed to find a window of opportunity to escape.

Robin nodded. "I didn't want to eat at first, I was worried it'd be drugged, like my water at the meet. But I got so thirsty . . ."

"You need to keep your strength up," Abby said. "We need to stay alert if we're going to get out of here."

She paced around the little shed, kicking at the walls again. She stood on her tiptoes and pressed her fingers against the ceiling, hoping there would be *some* spot with some sort of give. Anything.

He'd built this prison smart. Strong.

But he'd never kept two girls at once. He was out of his element here. Taking on a new challenge. There'd be a period of adjustment, where he'd be finding his footing, adjusting his rituals and precautions.

She needed to get him to make a mistake. Because the only way they were getting free was out that door. Which meant getting past him.

"What can you see out of the flap?" she asked Robin, who was scrunched down on the floor, her face pressed against the door, trying to peer through the gap.

"Just a lot of dirt," Robin said.

"No trees?" Abby asked.

"I think we might be at the bottom of a hill or something. I can't see the horizon," Robin said. "I . . ." She sucked in a quick breath. "Shit." She dropped the flap down, scrambling away from the door. "He's coming."

"Get behind me," Abby directed her, pointing to the far corner of the shed. She grabbed the bucket, ignoring the smell. It was her only weapon and she was gonna use it.

There was a scuttling sound, and then two plates full of what looked like canned beans and bread were pushed through the flap. She could hear a dim whistling sound.

That damn bastard was *whistling*.

Her temper flared and she marched over to the door, pounding on it with her fists. She bent down, pushing the flap on the door open, peering through it, trying to see anything.

"Hey!" she shouted through the flap. "I see you, you fucker! Why don't you come face me like a man?"

She could see his boots in the crack, heading away from her. Desperation spiked inside her and she thought about Zooey's theory earlier. That Dr. X and the unsub were related.

"Don't you want to hear what your father told me about you?" she yelled.

The boots stopped. *Yes.* Fear and panic, mixed with adrenaline flooded her as she leapt to her feet, gripping the bucket tighter in her hand. Robin hugged the wall, her fists clenched, ready to spring at Abby's signal.

Abby nodded to her. *Get ready.*

There was a scrape of the key in the lock. Then another.

One more . . .

The final lick clicked free, and the door swung open.

Abby squinted in the sudden light, her eyes tearing up.

"Oh, my God," Robin said behind her, when she saw who it was.

"You . . ." Abby breathed, her eyes widening.

She had no time to process it. No time to react. She had to attack.

She screamed. A warrior yell. A battle cry.

Swinging the bucket high, she charged.

CHAPTER 35

Y ou got anything yet?" Paul asked.

He'd spent a good ten minutes pacing around the little courtyard in front of the sheriff's station. He finally stopped when the woman who owned the coffee shop across the street came out with a cup of chamomile tea.

"You look stressed, sweetie," she'd told him with a motherly smile.

He didn't have the heart to tell her that no tea was going to help him. He'd just taken it with a thank-you and steeled himself to go back inside to see if Zooey had made any progress.

He needed to check on his family. He needed to check on Jonah, Abby's orchard manager. Abby would never let him hear the end of it if he didn't make sure her employees were being well treated. He needed to check in with Cyrus at the crime scene.

He needed Abby by his side, not lost, somewhere in those mountains, likely the only thing standing between his niece and a terrible fate.

God, he just wanted to sink into the ground and never get back up. But he couldn't.

If his sister lost her only child, Georgia would never recover. You didn't recover from something like that.

His mother had endured more than most in her life, but he knew she couldn't survive the death of her first grandchild.

He couldn't survive losing Robin.

He couldn't survive losing Abby.

So he was going to have to make sure that didn't happen.

Hang on, he thought. *Hang on. I am coming for you. I promise.*

He squared his shoulders, made sure his gun was securely holstered, and he went back inside.

"You find anything yet?" he asked.

Zooey shook her head. "I'm triangulating locations from the IP addresses of his posts, but I think he's got spoofing software to bounce the signal. I pulled up the Antaeus myth," Zooey said, rolling her chair back to the second computer she had set up. She had a pair of glasses on her head and a second pair on a chain around her neck, but wasn't wearing either. She tapped at a few keys, and then rolled back to the white-board.

"So Antaeus is a half giant. He's the son of Poseidon and Gaia. He's invincible, as long as he's connected to the ground, aka his mother. So he's this huge, famed fighter no one can defeat—until Hercules comes along. Hercules figures out Antaeus's weakness, and he lifts him *off* the ground, and crushes him."

"Yeah, I know this," Paul said.

"Antaeus is all about winning," Zooey said. "Remind you of anyone?"

"It's all a competition with this guy," Paul said disgustedly.

Zooey's black brows scrunched together. "It's a competition," she echoed, her eyes narrow-ing. And then they widened, almost comically huge and she smacked Paul hard across the shoulder with the notebook she was holding. "It's a competition!" she said again. "Boss, it's a *competition*!"

"Zooey, elaborate," he said. "My brain doesn't work as fast as yours."

"Competition! That's what the missing girls have in common. They were all athletes! I just didn't think it was important because they all did different sports so there was no crossover.

But what if the crossover wasn't the *sport*? What if it was the *coach*?"

The hair on the back of his neck stood up. "Wait, you mean . . ."

"When I talked to Dr. Jeffrey about what he remembered from the ME pages he gave to Sheriff Baker, he mentioned that on Cass's skin, he found traces of urethane."

Zooey was looking at him like she expected him to be blown away by this fact. "I don't know what that is."

"It's a chemical commonly used in cleaning supplies. Specifically, in the stuff they use to clean gym floors. Or, if you're a psychopathic killer and have it handy, it's the stuff you use to clean up after you've killed someone."

"Oh, my God." Paul reared to his feet, realization hitting him.

Robin's wrestling coach . . . the one who hadn't wanted her to join the team.

Coach Patten.

Coach Patten had coached Cass in softball all those years ago.

He coached the girl's soccer team, which is probably how Keira Rice got on his radar. He would've been a normal sight at sporting events around Northern California.

His chest tightened. His fingers itched for his gun.

Coach Patten was Dr. X's apprentice. All these years, he'd been sitting in Castella Rock High School's gym, the pick of his victims spread out in front of him. A steady stream of girls coming in and out from all over Northern California, as they competed against his teams.

It was like a fucking buffet to a sicko like him.

Paul's stomach clenched. His training was screaming at him to call the sheriff, to call the highway patrol, to call in his own team from DC.

But the time for training was gone.

Now?

It was time for action.

"Get Cyrus on the phone," he told Zooey. "Tell him we're going hunting."

CHAPTER 36

Abby came at Coach Patten swinging. The bucket cracked across his face, splitting in half with the force of her blow, spraying the contents everywhere.

"Robin! *Run!*" she yelled. The girl dashed past her and the wrestling coach, and Abby was right behind her as the man staggered toward her, dazed and spitting out whatever filth had splattered into his mouth.

"Go, go!" she shouted at Robin, who bolted. It was dark, she could barely see anything in front of her, but she slammed the shed door closed and darted after Robin, running up the hill. Her thigh muscles burned as she scaled the top of the hill, looking around frantically, trying to get *some* sort of sense of her surroundings. She registered the sky, trees in the distance, and a light in the distance—Patten's house.

"Get to the trees." She grabbed Robin's arm, wrenching the girl in the right direction. Even this far from the shed, she could hear a kicking sound.

Any second, he was going to kick down that door and come for them.

"Hurry, hurry," she urged Robin as they ran down the slope of the hill, disappearing into the tree line.

It was even darker in here, their every step a loud crackle as they moved deeper into the forest.

"Robin, find a weapon," Abby hissed. "A big rock. A stick. Anything you can use. Do *not* let go of it."

There was no way they were going to outrun him. This was *his* forest. This was his home.

They had to outsmart him. Surprise him.

Abby bent down, scooping up a long, thick branch that was more like a baseball bat. She hefted the weight of it in her hands, and then tossed it to Robin, who caught it.

"Come on." Abby pulled Robin through the woods, moving as fast as they could. Minutes passed, their panting breaths the only sound. But then she heard it: whistling.

"It's him," Robin whispered. She was shaking next to Abby, her grip on her makeshift club trembling.

Abby scanned the area, trying desperately to find something—a tree, a bush, a gully—to hide in. Somewhere he wouldn't easily find them.

The whistling was getting louder. They had to move. Now.

"Up the tree," Abby hissed, pushing Robin toward the old oak tree up ahead. "Climb it. Get out of sight. Keep hold of that stick."

She had to draw him away from Robin. If he was chasing her, he couldn't chase Robin. It was a temporary solution, one that'd likely get her killed, but it was the only one she had.

She'd be damned if he snuffed out another young life.

Robin scrambled up the tree, Abby handing her the club. "Don't move," she ordered. "Remember your martial arts training. I'm gonna draw him away from here and then I'll circle back."

She dashed away, dodging through the trees with her heart in her throat. She bent and scooped up another club for herself, holding it close to her chest as she moved as swiftly as she could.

She wasn't careful, crashing through the

underbrush, snapping twigs and branches, and catching her hair on bushes as she went. She wanted him to follow her, to be drawn to the noise she was making, not searching for Robin.

If she could just hold him off . . .

But as the ground beneath her feet started to climb, the forest floor steepening as she ventured farther into the mountains, a dreadful kind of surety began to fall over her.

For them to get out of this alive, Coach Patten had to go down.

And Abby had to make sure he wouldn't get back up.

Her fingers tightened around the club, and her lungs felt three sizes too small as she scaled the cliff overlooking the forest floor. She'd be able to see him coming from here.

But then he could see her too. She hesitated, flattening herself against a tree, torn.

No one was coming to save them. Paul . . . Paul didn't even know where they were.

Her heart thumped wildly. If she and Robin managed to outrun Patten, they'd end up so deep in the wilderness, it would likely kill them before he did.

She closed her eyes, searching the forest for any sounds of pursuit. She thought about her father, taking her out in the woods, the endless hours of quiet as they stalked deer. How careful he had been. How silent. How swift.

She needed to be like her father now.

She needed to be cautious.

She needed to be hard.

She needed to be fearless.

She heard him before she saw him, that damn whistling floating through the trees. She crawled belly down along the ground, to the very edge of the cliff that overlooked the forest floor. When he came into sight, she went very still, praying he wouldn't catch sight of her hair in the moonlight.

She watched as he drew closer. He was practically meandering. Hands in his pockets, whistling a jaunty tune, like he was on a pleasant evening stroll.

Her fingers clenched tight around the club, her feet digging into the fall leaves and dirt that covered the ground. Just . . . one . . . more . . . step . . .

There.

Abby sprang over the edge of the embankment, soaring through the air. Patten let out a surprised huff as she slammed into him from above, his body breaking her fall. They rolled along the forest floor, grappling for supremacy. He grabbed a chunk of her hair and ripped it from her head along with a scream from her throat. Then she spat in his face, scrabbling across the ground, searching for the club that had fallen from her hand.

"Bitch," he snarled at her, the first word he'd spoken.

Her fingers closed around a rock, and she swung up her arm and smashed it against his temple. It made him jerk back, his hold on her loosening. She wiggled out from under him, coughing and panting, spinning in a confused circle, trying to figure out which was what which.

"You couldn't leave well enough alone, could you?" Patten panted, getting to his feet.

Run, Abby's mind screamed.

"You've never been my type, Abigail," he said, his dark eyes glittering under the weak light of the moon pouring through the trees. "But God, you are persistent, aren't you? *Wah,* my best friend was killed. *Wah,* her killer isn't the right one! *Wah,* her boyfriend doesn't love me." He smiled mockingly at her. "You're such a child."

"Says the guy who keeps abducting teenage girls in a bid to prove a point to his daddy," Abby spat. He wasn't charging at her, he seemed almost relaxed, even with blood dripping down his forehead where she'd struck him with the rock. If she could keep him talking, at least he wasn't looking for Robin.

"My father has no nuance," Patten said, rolling his eyes. "He was a means to an end."

"He has plenty more to say about you," Abby said, licking her lips, trying to think fast. Patten was obsessed with proving himself to Wells, no matter what he said. They were obsessed with each other. That's why Wells had finally decided to see her. He'd finally decided to teach his son a lesson, through Abby.

"When you found him, did he tell you he didn't know about you?" She widened her eyes. She could do mocking too. "Did you really believe that lie? Of course he knew about you. But he didn't think you were good enough."

"Shut up!" Patten snapped.

"And then when you tracked him down, well . . . I guess he thought you had potential." She sighed, shrugging. "I guess great men do sometimes make mistakes."

"*I'm* the great man," Patten hissed. "He's a loser. I beat him," Patten said. "I always beat him."

"Yet here I am," Abby said.

She caught a sliver of movement over his shoulder in the darkness. She tried not to tense up when she saw the figure moving toward them. Patten was still facing her, determined to prove himself, and she had to keep it that way.

"You really think you've won this time?" Abby asked, trying not to stare too hard over his shoulder. Who *was* that? Had Paul somehow found them? Were he and Cy heading toward her right now? God, she hoped so. At any second, Patten was going to snap and go for her, and she couldn't outrun him.

"You're not getting out of this," Abby told him, her chin tilting up. "You can kill me, but they're gonna find you. You coached Paul Harrison. You know what kind of man he is. He doesn't give up. He'll find you." She waited a beat, her heart beating madly. "You've lost, Patten."

His eyes bulged and he lunged toward her, intent on killing.

But he had barely taken that first step toward her, when . . .

Wham!

The makeshift club arced through the air, clipping him on the back of the skull. His head whipped to the side, spittle and blood flying everywhere as he fell to the ground like a sack of potatoes, unconscious.

Robin loomed over him, the stick clutched tightly in her hand. "Weaker sex, my ass," the teen spat.

She raised her eyes—enormous pools of blue, brimming with tears—to meet Abby's shocked gaze. And then promptly started sobbing.

"Oh, honey," Abby said, hurrying over to hug her. "It's okay. It's okay. Thank you. That was amazing." She kept one eye on Patten's unconscious form. "We need to find rope or cuffs or chains or—"

"Robin?! Robin! *Abby!*"

She and Robin spun, Robin raising her club once again, a defensive move that was all instinct, as her adrenaline supply was supercharged.

Paul broke through the line of trees, coming to a halt when he saw the two of them.

"Uncle Paul!"

Robin dropped the club, rushing toward him. He swept her up in his arms, hugging her frantically, pushing her hair back, looking into her eyes, checking her pupils, firing questions at her that probably made her head spin.

Cyrus came hurrying down the embankment, a pair of cuffs in his hand. He bent down, securing them around the still-unconscious Coach Patten's wrists, then checked for a pulse.

"She didn't kill him," Abby said quickly.

"Robin did this?" Cyrus asked, looking impressed. "Guess you two didn't need our help," he said.

"We got lucky," Abby said, thinking about how scary it was, running through the woods. How she was sure it was going to be the last thing she ever did.

"Lucky? Smart, I'd say. Ambulance is en route," Paul said, trying to sweep Robin up in his arms.

His niece batted his hands away crankily. "I'm *fine*, Uncle Paul," she said, even though she still had tears tracing down her face. "Go check on Abby. She's the one who had to fight him. I just knocked him out."

Paul looked at Abby, his eyes saying everything. She wanted so badly to lean on him and she knew he was feeling the same, but they had Robin to think about. She was the priority here. They needed to get her to the hospital—and then home to her mom and dad.

She'd been through a deeply traumatizing experience. Abby was so relieved that Patten hadn't done anything to her beyond lock her in a shed. Who the hell knew what kind of torture the other girls he'd taken had suffered in the months—or years—he kept them there. She thought about that rusty red stain on the concrete floor of the shed, felt sick again, and looked down at Patten's prone body, wondering if she would be a terrible person if she kicked him a few times.

"Abby, she's right, come on," Paul said. "You need to get checked out."

"I'm fine," Abby insisted.

"You've got a cut on your calf that's bleeding all over," Robin said, pointing.

Abby looked down, surprised. There was a long, deep cut—probably from a branch or maybe from her swan-dive on top of Patten earlier—running down her leg.

"It doesn't hurt," she said.

"That's the shock," Paul said. "Come on. We need to get you out of the forest before the adrenaline fades and you start hurting."

"I'll stay here, make sure he doesn't go any-where," Cyrus said.

Abby hesitated, not really wanting to leave. The idea of letting him out of her sight—even for a second—made something creepy and hor-rible crawl up her spine.

"Don't worry," Paul said, and his hand was suddenly in hers, the touch giving her strength she didn't know she needed at that second.

She reached up and pressed her lips to his, not caring that Robin let out a little squeal when she did it—teenagers *were* resilient.

It was a quick kiss, a simple one lasting barely three seconds. But it made everything that had happened fade, just for a second when it was just him and her, and only them.

"Okay," she said, softly, pulling away. "Let's go."

ABBY WASN'T QUITE sure how they got to the hospital. By the time they had left the forest and saw the flashing lights of the ambulance heading down the road toward them, the adrenaline had started to ebb, and she was feeling distinctly spacey. She seemed to float from the ambulance to the hospital, where they stitched up her leg and tried to convince her to stay overnight.

"Absolutely not," she said, pointing at the IV in her arm. "Get this out of me. I want to go home."

"Abby." Paul sighed, shooing the nurses away with an apologetic look.

"Where is he?" she demanded. "Has the interrogation started? I want to watch. I need to know what he says about Cass."

"Abby," he said softly. "Sit. Breathe."

She pressed her lips together, annoyed. "I want to know," she insisted.

"And I want you to rest," he said. "Christ, I almost lost you."

She felt a flash of shame. She hadn't thought about how scary it must've been for him, to come back from the farmhouse to find her gone. She jerked up. "Roscoe!" she said. "Oh, my God, what happened to Jonah? Is he okay? Is Roscoe?"

"They're both fine," Paul assured her. "Jonah's got a bump on his head. Roscoe was wandering around the goat orchard. He's with my mom."

"Where's Robin now?" she asked. "Is she okay? Are Georgia and Jason here yet?"

"Robin's already with her parents. It's okay, Abby. You don't have to worry about anything. You just need to lie back and rest."

"I—" Abby bit her lip. "If I stop, I'm afraid I'm going to freak out," she confessed.

"Oh, honey." He pulled back her blankets, sliding into the bed next to her. She leaned into the solid length of his body, already feeling better as he wrapped her in his arms and cuddled her close. He kissed the top of her head.

"You saved Robin," he whispered. "I don't even know how to thank you."

"Actually, Robin saved *me*," Abby corrected him. "She's a total badass. When I was her age, I wouldn't have been brave enough to clobber him like that. She has the Harrison guts, clearly."

He smiled. "She wants to be an FBI agent."

Abby tilted her head, taking that in. "She'd be great," she said. "But Georgia's going to have a fit."

Paul laughed, brushing a kiss against her temple. "Please rest," he said. "For me."

She closed her eyes, telling herself she was just doing it to appease him. But he was so warm, and she felt so safe.

Abby fell asleep cradled in his arms, finally succumbing to the exhaustion, knowing he wouldn't let anything happen to her.

CHAPTER 37

Two weeks later

A re you ready?"
Abby nodded.
Stan, the prison guard, opened the door leading to Wells's section of solitary. She nodded as he pointed to the panic button like before.

"Thank you, Stan. I'll just be a few minutes," she said.

She waited until he had left, until it was just Wells and her, and only then did she turn to him.

There was still a fading bruise spreading across her temple. She had thought about trying to cover it with makeup, but she had a feeling that sort of effort would just delight Wells.

"You've come to see me again," Wells said.

"For the last time," Abby said.

He clucked. "You didn't bring Agent Harrison with you."

"He doesn't need to see you," Abby said. She admired that about Paul. That he didn't need this validation. That he didn't need to stand there and face him.

But Abby did.

"I had no idea I was so important to you."

"I found him," Abby said.

"I figured." Wells gestured to the mess of purple and green on her face. "Is that his handiwork?"

"You should see him," Abby said, a mean smile playing across her face.

Robin's blow to Patten's head had fractured his skull. It had taken a week for him to regain consciousness because of brain swelling. By then, the FBI had dismantled his entire home, finding trophies and items from not just the seven missing girls that Zooey had identified, but five other girls in Oregon whose remains were still unknown. Cadaver-sniffing dogs had gone through as much of Patten's property as they could, but who knew where they were buried. Who knew how many more stone Xs were hidden in the forest?

Cass hadn't been his first, but she'd been his most important—the kill that he kept trying to emulate over and over again. Abby had watched as he had waxed poetical about Cass, downplaying her athleticism and competitive spirit, going on and on about her femininity, how proud he'd been when she'd stopped playing softball. *A girl shouldn't try to be like the boys*, he'd told Agent Grace Sinclair, who had flown in specially to interview him before taking him to prison. *Cass came to understand that. I taught her that.*

The profiler's lip had curled, unable to hide her disgust as she concluded the interview.

"I hope you didn't hurt him too badly," Wells said. "Wouldn't that make you just like us?"

Abby snorted. That smile was back on her face. "I'm nothing like you two," she said. "I'm smarter."

Wells chuckled. "Quite the claim."

"I figured it out," Abby said. "Why you finally let me see you. Why you set this all in motion."

"It was time someone put him in his place," Wells said.

"It wasn't that at all," Abby said. She leaned forward. "You missed him," she said. "Your son. You wanted to see him. In order to do that, you had to expose him."

A smile curled across his face. "That would require quite a lot of sentiment on my part. Do you think I'm capable of such things, Abigail?"

"I think that for people like him, people like you? Exerting power over others is the closest thing you can get to love. You and him? You show each other you care by hurting each other. By taunting each other. By killing for each other. But now . . ." She trailed off.

Something flickered in Wells's eyes. "What did you do?" he asked.

"I won," Abby said. "I got justice for Cass. And I'll get justice for all his victims. But this?" She gestured to the empty room, to the loneliness that was awaiting him. "This is a favor to the other girls. The ones that *you* killed. The girls that you carved Xs into and stole their breath and their lives like you were entitled to them. For those girls, I give this gift: You will never, ever get what you most want. Your son will rot in prison on the other side of the state, and you will never see him again. Never talk to him again. We figured out how you were communicating. Those little letters of yours won't reach him again."

Wells was white as a sheet, staring transfixed at her.

"You vicious little thing," he said.

"I warned you before," Abby said. "Predators who mess with farm girls? We'll get you. Every time. You should have listened."

She walked out of the room without even looking back, feeling like a part of her was finally free. As she made her way out of the prison and to the parking lot, it felt as if a weight was finally lifted from her shoulders.

She loved Cass. She would always love her. Growing up as a girl was hard enough without a best friend, and she was glad Cass had been hers. Cass had been a good friend and a bad friend, and Abby had been the same in turn. They had made mistakes and they had made good choices and bad ones, because they were human and they had just been getting started.

Bert Patten had taken Cass away before she was able to soar. Abby would always hate him. It would always be a wound in her heart that Cass never got to grow up, to become who she was supposed to become. Now that wound was as healed as it ever was.

Abby had to let go. Finally lay Cass to rest. Leave behind the bad, cherish the good, and get past all the pain.

Abby walked into the prison parking lot. Paul was leaning against her truck, waiting.

She walked over to him, a soft smile on her face.

"You okay?" he asked, looping an arm around her waist and pulling her close.

She shook her head. "But I will be," she said.

He tucked a strand of her hair behind her ear,

tracing the line of freckles that lined the edge of her jaw. She looked at him, feeling settled in a way she never had experienced before.

"I love you, you know," he said.

She tilted her head up and they kissed, a slow, sweet kiss that she felt to the tips of her toes. The kind of kiss that started a forever.

They broke apart, just barely, her forehead still pressed to his, their chests brushing, her fingers winding in his hair and his in hers.

"I love you too," she whispered.

He smiled. "So . . . what are we going to do about that?"

She beamed. For a moment, she couldn't quite believe the boy next door and the girl across the meadow were finally standing in the same place, at the same time, their hearts finally free to truly love each other. But it was real and their time was here. Their future was forever.

Cass would have wanted them to seize it.

And so they would.

**Don't miss any of Tess Diamond's
riveting romantic suspense novels!**

DANGEROUS GAMES

In Tess Diamond's gripping debut, when an elite negotiator and a security expert team up to solve a kidnapping, the only thing higher than the tension is the heat . . .

Maggie Kincaid left the FBI two years ago and didn't look back . . . until now. A senator's daughter has been abducted, and the nightmare set in motion isn't just familiar to Maggie, it's personal. She'll need all the help she can get to bring Kayla Thebes home alive—even if that help comes from a hot-as-hell ex-soldier who plays by his own rules . . .

For Jake O'Connor, negotiation equals weakness. But he's immediately drawn to the sexy former agent who epitomizes strength. It isn't long before he and Maggie are working together 24–7, learning to read each other's signals and wanting much more.

But for Maggie and Jake, letting their guard down—even around each other—may be dangerous. Now, as they close in on a kidnapper with nothing to lose, their first mistake could shatter a young girl's last chance . . .

SUCH A PRETTY GIRL

In Grace Sinclair's bestselling crime novels, the good guys win and the bad guys always get caught. As the FBI's top profiler, she knows that real life is rarely so straightforward. But her new case isn't just brutal—it's also personal. The victims look like Grace. And the FBI recruit assigned to her team is trouble of another kind.

This isn't how Special Agent Gavin Walker imagined running into Grace again. Two years ago they shared one earth-shattering night, then she vanished from his life. She's brilliant, fiercely independent, and in mortal danger from a killer masterminding a twisted game . . .

The body count is rising. Entangled in the case and in each other, Gavin and Grace are running out of time and chances. And as Grace puts the pieces together, she knows she'll have to confront her own deepest secrets before the final, fatal move is played.

TESS DIAMOND

is a romantic suspense addict with a taste for danger—
and chocolate cake. She lives in Colorado Springs with
her law enforcement husband, two kids, and a ferocious
Jack Russell guard dog. She always dreamed of being an
FBI agent, and now she almost is—if watching *24* reruns
and plotting her next novel count.

www.avonromance.com
www.facebook.com/avonromance

ISBN 978-0-06-265584-4

In Tess Diamond's third romantic thriller,
an FBI agent teams up with the one woman
who can offer the salvation he needs
as they search for a serial killer . . .

As the head of an elite FBI unit, Special Agent Paul Harrison
seems to have everything figured out, but beneath the
surface, an internal war is raging. When he returns to his
rural hometown for the first time in a few years, he's faced
with the memories that led to his losing the love of his life.

Fifteen years ago, Abigail Winthrop's best friend, and
Paul's girlfriend, was murdered by the infamous serial killer
Dr. X. Now an investigative journalist, she's determined
to find the truth. But when Abigail discovers evidence that
clears Dr. X, she realizes the real killer is still out there and
is striking again when local young girls begin disappearing.

Turning to Paul for help, Abigail joins forces with him.
As an undeniable attraction develops between them,
they must heal deep wounds from their past—and find
a relentless psychopath who could extinguish their
hopes for a future together.

An Avon Romance

Available from HarperCollins e-books

DISCOVER GREAT AUTHORS, EXCLUSIVE OFFERS, AND MORE AT HC.COM.

ISBN 978-0-06-265584-4

0418

5 0 7 9 9

EAN

9 780062 655844

AVON BOOKS
Win free prizes, get exclusive content,
and more—scan with a QR App now!

Romance | USA $7.99 CAN $9.99